Magic Misrule

The Raven Academy Book Three

A. Caprice

Cover Art by Dar Albert

Chapter One

"Does he have it?"

Gareth gave a long-suffering sigh. "If he had it, he would end his travels."

I peeled open one gummy eye. Dante's body still floated inches above Gareth's and my joined hands. His eyes were closed, his face serene. Like he'd astral-traveled to a farkin' island getaway instead of Arzrigoth where he was supposed to be.

My shoulders sagged and I closed my eye again, trying to concentrate on the spell. An island beach sounded awesome right about now. When we got Bane back, and after we'd saved the world, of course, maybe I could convince my guys to take me on a vacay.

Gareth squeezed my hand. The magic flowing between us thickened, his strength shoring up my wavering reserves.

I was exhausted. It had been eight days since Bane had disappeared.

Been taken.

Eight days of Gareth searching the different worlds and dimensions. Of Dante using every contact from his white lodge, trying to trace Bane's whereabouts. Of me, Hazel, and Quincy searching every damn book in the library for a reference to any spell that could possibly make someone's consciousness disappear but didn't mean he was dead.

Because I refused to believe that Bane was dead. I'd feel it if he was. I'd know.

And maybe I was just fooling myself. Because it had been eight days and we'd found nothing. He'd vanished without a trace. Like he'd been...

I swallowed, the back of my throat burning. If the members of Raven's council hadn't gone into hiding, I would have taken great pleasure in beating every single one of them into a bloody pulp until the one who'd betrayed Bane confessed to what he'd done.

"Focus," Gareth murmured.

I tried. We were working a spell that channeled our energy to Dante, allowing him to travel farther than most astral projections allowed. But I couldn't remember the last time I'd slept, my left butt cheek was going numb from sitting cross-legged on my bedroom floor for so long, and I was missing Bane so much my heart actually ached. Concentration was a bit hard to come by.

Gareth rubbed his thumb over mine, sending a comforting tingle along my skin. He'd said the more we touched, the better. Magic was like a network, and the greater the number of connections you had, the stronger it was.

I straightened my spine, sending all my intention into Dante to find Bane. This was a long shot, but it was our last shot. Gareth had convinced a Nahwalli demon, (and I didn't want to know how he did his convincing), to tell him about a rumored underground prison. One that was built to hold the magical. One that hadn't been authorized by any known government.

It sounded like the perfect place a rogue council of witches would send someone they wanted to disappear. Bane had to be there. Now we only needed to figure out where the damn prison was located.

The air shimmered, and my eyes flew open to see Dante's body vibrating. I moved to pull my hand from Gareth's, but he only tightened his grip.

"Don't disturb him now," he said. "Not when he seems to be getting somewhere."

Dante's lip curled in a grimace.

"But..." Astral projection shouldn't hurt. At least, I didn't think so. I'd never done it. But ever since Bane had been taken, my heart had clogged my throat whenever Gareth or Dante were in even the tiniest hint of danger. I couldn't bear to lose someone else I lo— cared about.

Dante panted, the sound loud, animalistic. His incisors stretched, growing long and pointy, and a shiver danced down my spine. I still wasn't used to the fact that one of my lovers was a vampire, and that his bite had been one of the most amazing experiences of my life. But I was getting there.

He snarled, snapped at the air.

"Gareth..."

"Wait."

Dante's nails extended, and my pulse rabbited. "We need to stop this."

"Just wait."

I bounced my knees, nervous energy rushing through my body. This really couldn't be good.

Dante's body spun, like a pig on a spit. When he faced me, his eyes flew open. They were slits, inhuman. He reached for me, those creepy, long nails stretching for my face, and I couldn't restrain a little shriek.

"No." The word was a low growl, barely audible over the thudding of my heart. But it was enough.

Dante blinked at Gareth's command, his gaze clearing. "What…?" He crashed face first to the floor, pinning Gareth's and my hands beneath him.

I tugged my hands free and flexed my fingers. "Are you okay? Did you find him? Where is he?"

Gareth rolled to his feet and stepped over Dante's body. "Give the pup a moment to collect himself. Astral travel is challenging for those less powerful."

Dante rolled to his back and glared up at the demon. "There is no world where I'm less powerful than you."

Gareth smirked. "Whatever you need to tell yourself."

I clapped my hands. "Focus. Where's Bane?" I stared at Dante, willing him to give me an answer I wanted to hear. I wouldn't accept that he hadn't found the prison, that our magic hadn't worked.

Dante gave me a sympathetic look, but that could mean anything. That I was having a bad hair day. That he felt sorry for me that I couldn't choose between my guys. Just because he wasn't answering didn't mean... Oh God. Had he not found the prison? Or had he found it and Bane wasn't in it? Or wasn't alive in it?

My mind raced so hard it went light. I planted a palm on the ground to hold myself steady. "Dante..."

He gripped my shoulder. "I found it. But it won't be easy getting inside."

If it weren't for his hand holding me upright I would have collapsed to the floor with relief. "That's not a problem." Nothing was a problem, not with Bane alive. "I like it hard." Because that meant they had a chance to get Bane back.

Gareth cleared his throat.

Dante smothered his smile.

I ran my words through my head again. My cheeks heated. "Jeez, grow up guys. That wasn't what I meant." Though, yeah, I liked it hard that way, too.

I stood, turning my focus on what needed to be done. "So, we have a location."

Dante nodded.

"And we know the security measures the prison uses."

Gareth shrugged. "We know some of them. My contact could have missed something."

"It doesn't matter. If something comes up, we'll deal with it." I swung my arms back and forth, getting blood flowing through them. I bobbed on my feet hoping if my body felt energized, my mind would, too.

Gareth tilted his head, his gaze dropping to my bouncing boobs. "What are you doing?"

"Getting ready."

"You want to launch a prison break now?" A curving line of blank ink slithered up Gareth's forearm and disappeared under the sleeve of his tee. I was getting better at interpreting the movements of his tattoos, and I think that one meant he wasn't a fan of my idea.

Too bad.

"Yes. Now." We'd need to stop by Gareth's gym and load up on weapons. After that, there was no reason to stall. "I'm not waiting one more minute than necessary to bring Bane back home."

Dante ran his hand up the back of his head, ruffling his hair. "Perhaps we should get a good night's rest and plan our attack tomorrow."

I swiveled my head to face him. "We know our plan. You create a portal to as close to Bane as possible, we grab him, we leave. Now that we know where this prison is, we can put our plan into effect."

"But—"

"No buts." I shook my head. "We're not going to learn anything more about the security systems. There will be no perfect moment. We go now."

Gareth dipped his head in agreement.

Dante clambered to his feet, blowing out a breath. "I don't like it, but I know you won't agree to anything else. Let's do it."

"Want any help?"

I peered around Gareth's ripped body, a grin stretching my lips when I saw Hazel and Quincy standing in my doorway.

Hazel sauntered into the room, Quincy quietly closing the door after them. "So the spell worked?" she asked. "We know where Professor Bane is?"

I nodded. "We're bringing him home."

"Is it wise involving them?" Gareth's tone wasn't unkind, but it was measuring when he looked at my friends. And obviously he found something lacking.

I grabbed a dark hoodie and shrugged it on. "They have better control of their magic than I do, and we can use all the help we can get." I didn't like risking my friends' lives, but we were past the point of such concerns. A war was coming, and without Bane, I didn't like our chances of winning. How many friends were going to die in the battle?

No, the stakes were too high to let my protective instincts get in the way. I strode for the door. "Let's go. If anyone wants extra weapons beside their magic, we'll load up at Gareth's. I call dibs on the battle axe."

I didn't wait to see who followed.

I had a man to rescue.

Chapter Two

"I'm so sorry," Hazel said for the hundredth time.

I squeezed the handle of my battle axe and watched the shimmering rectangle Dante had disappeared into. "Don't worry about it."

Gareth stood next to me, arms crossed, his lips twitching in amusement. The bastard.

Quincy had eased to stand well away from Hazel and me, getting out of the danger zone of any potential blow-up.

"I don't understand it." Hazel picked up the end of my ponytail and rubbed the violet strands between her fingers. "I've performed the coloring spell on my sister many times." She frowned. "It must be because your hair was already chemically treated. It messed with my magical coloring."

I took my hair and shoved it back beneath my black hoodie. Hazel had been right that I shouldn't attempt a prison breakout with attention-getting bright blue hair, and for once I'd been willing to go back to my natural, boring brown. But Hazel's spell had gone just a bit awry.

"It's fine." I squinted. Was that a figure shimmering in the portal? My shoulders dropped. Nope. Just my eyes watering from lack of sleep. "The hood works just as well for camouflage."

"I can—"

Dante stepped from the portal, interrupting whatever idea Hazel had next.

I leapt forward, dragging him fully into the room. "Did you work it right? Does the portal take us to Bane?"

He nodded. "It opens in a supply closet down the hall from his cell. Most everyone is sleeping now. If we're going to go tonight, it should be now."

I nodded and turned for the gateway. I was done waiting to get Sinjin Bane back.

Gareth gripped my shoulder and nudged me away from the opening. "Me first, pet. We don't know what's waiting for us on the other side." He stepped into the glinting void and disappeared.

I huffed. Okay, *now* I was done waiting. My feet picked up speed. I leapt through the portal, and bounced off Gareth's back on the other side.

He turned from a door that was cracked open and pressed his finger against his lips.

I nodded and shuffled to the side so no one would knock into me.

By the time Gareth deemed it safe enough to go, Dante, Hazel, and Quincy had filled the small closet with us. It was a tight squeeze, and my axe *might* have cut a small wedge off of Hazel's black bob. But since I'd been so forgiving about her screw up with my hair, she'd have to be, too.

Gareth opened the door just enough to slip out. We all followed. I could feel the power humming between us, each of us ready to launch our spells. We were like guns with the safeties off. And with hair triggers. It was almost disappointing when we reached Bane's cell without having to use magic.

I rubbed the small, grimy window on the steel door. "Are you sure this is his cell?" I whispered. "I can't—"

A face pressed against the inside of the window, one piercing blue eye glaring out. It softened when it caught sight of me.

"Bane." His name was a prayer on my lips. I dug my fingers into the door, my breasts pressing against the cold metal, wanting to get as close as possible to him.

Gareth plucked me up and set me aside. "We'll get him out faster if you aren't dry-humping the door."

I would have been embarrassed if I wasn't so damn happy. I bounced on my toes while Gareth ran his hand over the locks, chanting under his breath. When the door finally swung open, I elbow-checked my demon aside and threw myself into Bane's arms.

He buried his face at my throat, inhaling deeply. I ran my hands over his body, checking for holes as I let his heat warm the cold pit of fear in my gut that had formed when he'd disappeared.

"You're alive," I breathed. Alive, and whole, and, okay, not smelling great, but who cared about that when he was finally letting me hold him like I'd always wanted? "I knew you were alive. Didn't I tell you?" I glared over my shoulder at Gareth and Dante.

"I didn't realize that fact had been in question." Bane's sexy English accent rolled over me and I wanted to do nothing but stay in his arms listening to it for hours.

"And if we want to keep it that way, perhaps we should get a move on?" Dante suggested.

Quincy nodded in agreement and peeked his head out the door. "Coast's clear."

"Get this damn thing off me." Bane pulled back and tugged at a bronze collar around his neck.

I reached for it but Gareth drew my hand away. "What is it?" I asked.

"A magic suppressor." Dante raised his index finger and a zing of green electricity zipped from the end and hit the collar. It fell to the floor in two pieces.

Bane raised his hands and a relieved expression crossed his face when magic flowed between his palms. "Thank God."

"Um, we have a problem." Hazel stepped back from the door. "A row of guards just made a formation at the end of the hall. I think they know we're here."

Bane smiled grimly. He cracked his neck. "I hope the ginger guard is among them. I owe that bastard some bruises." He strode for the cell door. "Ms. Willowtree, Mr. Quincy, please remain here until it's safe." Blue orbs of electricity popped up around his hands as he stepped into the hallway. Gareth and Dante were hot on his heels.

Hazel raised an eyebrow, giving me a look. “Until it’s safe?”

I shrugged. Hazel wasn’t impressed when Bane got all assertive, but I thought it was hot. Most of the time.

A high-pitched shriek sounded in the hall, and I gave my axe a twirl. “Let’s go.”

A thick mist blurred my vision. One of the walls was charred and smoking, and so was the left side of one of the guards. From the way he curled into a ball and rocked back and forth, I assumed he was the girly-shrieker.

My men were outnumbered, two or three guards for each of them. I stepped forward to enter the fray only to pause. I eyed the axe, then the soft flesh of the opposing warlocks.

I couldn’t do it. Couldn’t hack into witches. It had been easy when I’d been fighting tentacled monsters and undead beings. But this was different.

With a frustrated growl, I chucked the blade of the axe into the nearest wall and loaded up my next best weapon: my magic.

I dredged up my bitch-a-tude, the mindset that seemed to power my magic best. Seeing my three guys under fire made it easy.

I levitated the asshole who had put Dante in a chokehold and threw his body against the wall like I was beating a rug.

Hazel darted to my right and threw up a shield, the burst of magic a guard shot our way bouncing off of it.

Quincy leapt to my left side, hands raised. The guard who got in the way of his magic stiffened. His limbs shook then twisted around themselves like a pretzel. He fell to the ground and contracted in on himself.

I pursed my lips. Quincy would have to teach me that spell.

Pain rocketed up my side. I stopped admiring my friend's magic and concentrated on my own. Fortunately, the angrier I got, the less I had to think about my spells. They came instinctively.

A guard flew backwards when my spell hit him, a large round hole piercing the center of his uniform. And a part of his chest.

I swallowed back bile. The downside was my magic got a teensy bit out of control when I was pissed.

But I couldn't worry about that now. Two more guards turned the corner into the hallway. I threw out a cage, surrounding them with fiery bars.

One of the men had hair to match my cage.

Bane turned on him with a narrow-eyed glare. He bared his teeth. "That one's mine."

I didn't have time to watch what Bane did to the guard. I was too busy trying to keep myself and Quincy and Hazel alive. But I heard the screams.

Finally, the shrieks, the sounds of body hitting body, it all dwindled until they died out to nothing. The six of us stood, a little bruised and bloody but mostly unharmed, and looked at the guards scattered on the ground. Some of them moaned, but most were unconscious.

At least, I hoped they were only unconscious.

I hurried to the guard I had blasted in the chest and dropped to my knees. "Is he breathing?" I hovered my hand over his mouth, hoping to feel air moving. "I think he's breathing."

Bane took my arm and pulled me to standing. "It doesn't matter. We have to go."

"It matters to me." I'd only ever killed a person accidentally. Otherwise, it had been things that weren't quite human. Weird monsters. Shifters in their wolf forms. Maybe it didn't speak well for my character, but I could still sleep at night when the lives I took didn't look like me. I knew the guard wouldn't give me the same consideration, but I wanted him to live. "Please."

Bane blew out a breath. Shaking his head, he squatted and held his hands over the guard's charred uniform. A faint gold light shimmered in the space between Bane's hands and the man's chest. "He lives. Barely." He took several more breaths before rising. "I've given him enough healing energy that he should last until his friends arrive with medical help. It's all we can do."

I nodded, letting Dante take my hand and lead me back to the closet and our portal. I gave the guards, and the destruction we'd wrought, one last glance before turning the corner.

Bane was right. This was war. There was only so much we could do for our enemies.

But I didn't have to like it.

Chapter Three

I woke up the next morning to chaos. Despite Bane's reassurances that he was fine, I'd insisted on spending the night in his rooms. I'd eyed his bed hopefully, and he'd given me a stack of blankets and told me to make myself at home on the couch if I was going to be stubborn.

Well, the joke was on him because his couch was super comfy. Not as luxurious as Dante's bed, and the thought that I could have been snuggled up with at least one of my men on that amazing mattress did cross my mind a time or two during the night. But I'd been cozy all the same.

When I stepped outside of Bane's door, the first sign that something was wrong was the sight of Professor Paca dragging two tubs of ten-foot-tall banana trees down the hall.

"Professor, do you need any help?" The man didn't even glance at me as he stumbled past, eyes round and focused on the stairs at the end of the hallway.

Bane stood next to me, closing his door. "What's wrong?"

"Um, nothing I guess." My stomach growled. "Except I want breakfast."

"You and your stomach." Bane shook his head, his lips twitching. He turned, his step a bit slower than usual. He'd said he was unharmed during his imprisonment, but he looked like a faded version of himself.

I was tempted to reach for his hand as we walked. But aside from that one hug he'd allowed in his cell, Sinjin Bane had returned to his professor/student boundaries. Although he did seem a tad warmer. Perhaps his imprisonment had made him realize our relationship was more important than his professionalism. A girl could hope.

We hit the second floor, and a witch sprinted past us shrieking, reaching for two bats who flitted just out of her reach.

Bane rested his hand on my elbow before I could turn for the stairs to the ground floor. He strode to the far railing and looked down from the balcony onto the academy's great room. His eyes narrowed, and I rushed to his side.

"What the—"

Bane grabbed my wrist and dragged me down the hall. "We need to speak with Dreadmoon."

I was pulled along, looking back at the blue smoke wafting to the ceiling of the great room. "But what was—"

"Doesn't matter."

He pushed open the door to the outer office of the headmistress. Two filing cabinets lay on their sides, slips of paper escaping from the scattered folders and flying about the room. Bane ignored them as he hustled to the inner office, but I reached out to try to grab one of the origami birds.

The bastard pecked my hand, giving me a papercut.

"Son of a..." I shook out the sting, feeling more animosity toward a piece of paper than anyone should. "What is going on?" I trailed Bane into Dreadmoon's office. "It's like the whole school has gone mad."

"Not mad, Miss Jones." The headmistress stood next to a frame on the wall, one that used to hold a mirror.

I peered at it, then at the office. It definitely wasn't reflecting anything, but there was another room past it that looked like it belonged in a dollhouse.

"In fact, we're all finally getting smart," she continued. "Ever since you arrived at the Raven Academy, the situation has become more and more unstable." Holding out her hands, she levitated books from one of her shelves through the frame. "I've just heard from the Board of Overseers. The council members have disappeared. The school is no longer protected. Most professors agree it's time to leave."

Bane crossed his arms. "The council hasn't disappeared. They're fleeing. The white lodges have some questions for them."

Dreadmoon grabbed a wide leather satchel. "You don't really believe this rumor that the council has gone dark? I've worked with those witches and warlocks for years—"

"Council member Judah drugged my tea and transported me to Arzrigoth." Bane's nostrils flared. "I can only imagine that our years of friendship had him exile me instead of kill me." His knuckles went white around his biceps. "The council has chosen a side, and it is the wrong one."

Dreadmoon shifted uneasily. “If you were drugged, your memory of events probably isn’t accurate. And you might have been sick instead of drugged.” She shook her head, setting the feathers dangling from her ears swinging. “I won’t believe my colleagues have turned without proof.”

“But—”

Bane held up a hand, cutting me off. “Don’t bother.”

“But she has your word.” I frowned. “Plus all the attacks that have happened here at the academy, the attempts on my life. The prophecy. Isn’t that proof enough?”

Dreadmoon turned her back and plucked up a patchwork vest from the back of her chair. She shrugged it on.

“Some people won’t acknowledge the truth until it steps up and slits their throat,” Bane said. “We won’t convince her. Don’t waste your time.”

I gritted my teeth as the headmistress trotted to the wall. She turned before the frame. “I wish you both well, but I would urge you to leave Raven, at least until things get sorted with the council.” She pinned Bane with a look. “No job is worth this.” And with a brisk nod, she faced the frame, leaned forward, and was sucked into the wall, appearing as a smaller version of herself on the opposite side. The figure waved her hand, and the image of her room disappeared, leaving me staring at my own reflection, a tousle of violet hair surrounding my indignant face.

"Her job?" I couldn't keep the disgust out of my voice. "You just barely escaped with your life, the council has essentially declared war, and she thinks this about her job?"

Bane took my hand and rubbed his thumb over my knuckles. The tension in my shoulders eased. "It's safer for her right now to keep her head buried in the sand. Unfortunately, soon that will no longer be the case. I fear the war Druella foretold is upon us."

I stared at his hand, a shade darker than my own. His nails weren't the even trim they usually were, but torn and uneven. Like he'd tried to claw his way out of prison.

I turned my hand to more fully clasp his own. A chill stole my breath. It was really happening. A war between the magical worlds. I'd thought I'd believed it, but it had never really sunk into my bones. But now I knew.

The war was inevitable. People were going to die. And it was up to me to save as many as I could.

Bane straightened his fingers, tried to tug his hand away.

"Don't," I said.

"Delaney." He blew out a breath. "This can never happen."

"Why?" Dante and Gareth gave me so much, but I felt incomplete without Bane, too.

"I'm a professor; you're a student."

"The Raven Academy isn't operating anymore," I reminded him. "That excuse doesn't work."

"We're facing the end of our world."

"Yes, and we might die." I cupped my other hand below his, encompassing it fully. "All the more reason to enjoy life while we have it."

These were all kick-ass arguments, if I did say so myself, and I could see the indecision on Bane's face.

His mouth settled into a grim line. "Your bed is a bit too crowded for my liking, Miss Jones. Perhaps when you have a vacancy, we can revisit the issue. Until then, I think it's best we concentrate on stopping this war, don't you?"

My breath whooshed out of me as my lungs squeezed tight. I dropped his hand like it was on fire.

Right. Of course. Gareth and Dante were already wigged out by my being with both of them. What man would want to join in with that shit show?

The backs of my eyes burned, but I refused to cry. I lifted my chin. "You're right. Our focus should be on stopping what's coming. We should find Gareth and Dante and talk strategy."

Without waiting for a response, I turned on my heel and strode from the room. I swiped my cheek with the back of my wrist before he fell into step beside me.

He sidestepped as a student raced past us on the stairs. "I'll talk with the other professors. See who's staying and who's left."

I nodded and crossed the great hall. The baby dragon that had been the cause of all that smoke sadly was no longer there.

I could use a good snuggle with a cute, purple dragon. Or have it bite my head right off and end my humiliation with one snap. Either outcome was fine by me right now.

I headed for the cafeteria, which seemed to be the destination of most students. Hopefully Hazel, Quincy, and Dante would be among them. I stopped at the entrance, my eyes widening. "What the...?"

A group of students sat on the floor eating cereal dry from its boxes. Another group played monkey in the middle with a delicious-looking croissant. And most concerning of all, the buffet table where my daily dose of caffeine was kept, was empty.

"No coffee?" I whined. If ever a morning needed coffee, it was this one.

"Cook's gone." Hazel wandered up to me nibbling a banana. "The students have raided the pantries."

My least favorite student marched up to me, her face flushed. "Not only is the cook gone, but apparently I am, too. My parents have ordered me home. What did you do?" she asked me accusingly.

"Not everything is because of me, Ophelia." Although, yeah, this one might be if the chaos was happening because of the stupid prophecy coming true. Though I really didn't see how it was my fault I was named as the bringer of destruction or light in a decades-old prophecy. As far as I was concerned, the blame rested fully on Fate's head.

"Can I have everyone's attention." Bane's voice echoed in the cavernous space. He stood on a table near the center of the cafeteria, his hands on his lean hips.

A couple students glanced his way, but most carried on as usual.

He heaved a sigh and held his hands up. His lips moved, blue energy gathering between his palms. Lightning and thunder erupted above our heads.

That quieted everyone down pretty damn quick.

"If I can have your attention for just a moment," he said with a small smile, but exhaustion weighted his features. "There is some turmoil at Raven and we need to address it. As you might have noticed, many professors are leaving the academy."

A student shouted from the corner, "My parents said Headmistress Dreadmoon was leading a cult and they're running to avoid being arrested."

Bane scrubbed his palm over his jaw. "Er, no. That's not what happened."

"It's the nephilim," another student said knowingly. "They've finally decided to end their banishment on their own terms and are coming for us."

"Nephilim?" I asked Hazel.

"Descendants of fallen angels," she whispered. "They tried to overthrow Lucifer. It didn't end well for them."

I nodded. I needed to create a spreadsheet for all this shit. Or maybe a Google Doc, one that Hazel had access to and could fill in—

"No," Bane barked. "None of your wild conspiracy theories." He crossed his arms over his chest. "The truth is this: the council of Raven Academy has joined forces with a dark enemy, providing him with mercenary witches in order to form an army intent on starting a war that could end in the destruction of all magical beings."

Hazel snorted, and I had to agree. Bane's explanation sounded like the biggest conspiracy theory of them all.

There was dead silence for a moment, then the loud buzz of excited whispering.

Bane raised his hand. "I know this comes as a shock..."

The chattering grew louder.

"...but it does no good shielding you from the truth..."

The students ignored him, some pulling out their phones, others huddling together in groups.

I put two fingers between my lips and whistled.

Hazel, Quincy, and Ophelia clapped their hands over their ears. "Jesus," Hazel said. "Warning next time?"

I mouthed 'sorry' to her before hurrying to Bane's table. I clambered on top of it and faced the now silenced room. "Hey, we don't have time for gossip. This isn't a joke. It isn't a game." I scanned the faces of my audience. Three months ago I hadn't known anyone here. And now I had to tell them that some of them would most likely die.

My stomach cramped. "Some of you know me. Some of you blame me for all the weird shit that's been going on since I arrived."

Ophelia smirked at that.

I took a deep breath. "And you're right. All the accidents and explosions and attacks happened because I came here. Because of what my presence foretold."

The cafeteria was completely still.

"Forty-two years ago there was a prophecy," I said. "One that said there was going to be a war to end all wars. Think World War Two, but for witches."

Bane huffed out a breath.

"You might not have heard of it, but your parents definitely have." I looked to Bane. "Right?"

"Yes, but the comparison to World—"

"How are you involved?" Ophelia asked.

I swallowed. This was it. It felt like I was getting naked on stage. Baring myself completely. "I was named in the prophecy. As the witch who would either save the world...or destroy it."

I waited for the shocked murmurs to subside. "Obvs, I want to be on the side that does the saving, but I'm going to need your help."

Bane shifted, his finger grazing my hand.

"We need your help," I amended. "Because the war is coming. The enemy's minions have been sent to kill me, to stop me from fulfilling the prophecy. Thanness was one of them." A shiver worked its way down my spine at the memory of the former student. Of how he'd created his own army of undead things, and tried to include Hazel and Quincy as his foot soldiers.

Of how I'd killed him.

I cleared my throat. "And so were the Bastardo brothers." I glanced at Ophelia, feeling some sympathy. Finding out the guys you were crushing on were murderous a-holes couldn't be easy.

"Someone is forming an army," Bane said. "An army of our former students. Of witches and shifters and demons. We don't yet know who is behind this. But we will."

Something shifted inside me; clicked. And I knew what we needed to do. "Yes, someone is forming an army. We need to form one, too."

Bane lowered his mouth to my ear. "They're students."

"Yes. So am I. So were the witches who have joined the other army." I shook my head. "I don't think the battle will spare them. They can hide, maybe survive for a couple months longer. Or they can fight to secure their future."

His shoulders sagged. "They're *my* students. *My* responsibility." But he knew I was right. I could see it in his eyes. And it was killing him.

My fingers itched to reach up and cup his jaw. But that wasn't my place. Bane didn't want it to be my place. So I gave him my best encouraging smile instead. "And we'll soon see how well you taught them. If they decide to join us."

I turned back to the crowd. "I know you'll need to think about this. You'll need to talk with your family. But war is coming, make no mistake. And if you want to fight against those who would destroy us, we'll be meeting in the gym this afternoon to train. To prepare for what lies ahead."

My stomach rumbled loudly, breaking the somber moment.

Ophelia shook her head and stomped out of the cafeteria. The other students started talking among themselves again, shooting me looks I couldn't decipher. Was I the crazy lady screaming about the end of the world? Or would they believe me? Only time would tell.

I hopped down and raised a hand to Bane.

He ignored it and jumped down himself. But he did wobble a bit on the landing.

"You need more rest," I told him.

"I need to start making calls. If we're going to form this army of yours, we're going to need more fire-power than the students at Raven." He stalked off, threading his way through the crowd and out of the cafeteria.

Hazel and Quincy joined me. "An army, huh?"

"Well, probably more like a small battalion." My head went light at all the implications. Would I just be providing proverbial cannon fodder for the enemy? I pushed away that unpleasant thought. There would be casualties. Maybe me. Maybe someone I cared about. But we had to fight anyway. And I would have to live with the consequences.

"Come on," I said, turning to more pressing matters. "Let's go see if there's anything left in the kitchen to raid."

Chapter Four

"What do you mean you're leaving?" I gaped at Gareth, not believing my ears. Gareth, Dante, and I were in Gareth's gym, me watching as he plucked his favorite weapons from his wall of sharp-and-pointy awesomeness and placed them in a large duffel bag.

"I've been summoned." He lifted one shoulder. "I have to go."

"Summoned to hell?" Dante ran his hand up the back of his head. "That's an invitation I'd RSVP no to."

Gareth buffed a sai with a soft, black T-shirt before adding it to his bag. "It's not so bad. Besides, I can nose around. See if I can learn anything that will help.

The person behind all this might be covert, but the ten members of the council aren't. If there's information to be had, the scavengers down in lower world will know it."

"I need you." I rubbed my palms on the thighs of my jeans. "We're meeting in the main gym in an hour. To form an army." I tried to impress upon him the importance of the event. "You're a big part of that."

"Sorry, pet." He zipped his bag and slung it over one shoulder. "You'll have to train your recruits yourself."

"But..." I'd sort of envisioned Gareth as my new army's drill sergeant, scaring everyone into discipline. Bane would be the general, devising strategy. Dante would be the friendly staff sergeant that everyone could turn to when things got rough.

And I would be... Well, I liked to imagine myself as the Hulk in the Avengers. Ready to be called up to beat the tar out of someone on command. But chances were I'd be more Private Benjamin, providing comic relief.

And just thinking that had me wanting to curl up on a sofa and watch 80s movies instead of dealing with the fate of the world. I thought I could handle it with my guys at my side, but now one of them was abandoning me.

I crossed my arms over my chest and tapped a toe. "You need to call your dad back and reschedule."

Gareth's lips twitched. "Reschedule with Lucifer?" He stepped up to me and gripped the back of my neck. "I *am* sorry. But you'll do fine."

"Then take me with you," I blurted out. Gareth looked surprised at my request, but not as surprised as I felt. I really didn't want to go to hell.

I snuck my finger through a belt loop on his jeans. But I really, really didn't want to spend another week of my life wondering if one of my men was hurt. Or dead. If Gareth was going to visit dear old dad, then I was going to.

Besides, it would make me feel better about my own father. I mean, he sucked, but not fire-and-brimstone levels of suck-itude. My childhood would look positively rosy in comparison.

Gareth's face went uncharacteristically soft. He cupped my cheek. "I'll be fine. And I couldn't take you with me even if I wanted to. Lucifer's palace has strong wards. Since I've been summoned, it will be calibrated to let me through, but not you."

I frowned. "But you've snuck in there before without an invitation. Can't I go the same way?"

He bent and teased my lips with his. "No. There is only one weakness in the shield. It reboots once every twenty-six hours. In that split second, someone can slip through. If you miss that window by even a fraction of a moment, you'd be killed. It recycled six hours ago, and I have to leave now. I can't wait twenty more hours to take you. Not that I'd ever willingly take you to lower world."

I opened my mouth to protest, but he covered my lips with his own. He deepened the kiss, and I forgot why I was arguing.

It took Dante's loudly cleared throat to bring me back to reality.

We broke apart, but didn't go far. I stared into Gareth's golden eyes, inches from my own, and wondered: would this be the last time I saw those eyes? Or would the next time we parted be the last? Is this what war was like, always questioning if you would see the other person again?

The frustration and fear swirling in my chest were almost enough to get me to admit my feelings. That somewhere along the way, my caring for these men had deepened into—

No. I stepped back, slamming the door on that idea. Indulging in it would do no one any good. If one of us didn't survive the war, it would only increase the feeling of loss. And if by some miracle we all did make it through, well, I still wasn't built for love. It was a skill some people just didn't learn. Or were never taught.

"Be safe," I told him.

Gareth nodded. He glared at Dante. "Take care of her."

I almost smiled. That must have cost him.

Dante's shoulders rounded. "I hate to say it, but I should go, too. My lodge wants to hold a conference with the other white lodges and they want me to speak. I need to meet with my employer and prepare."

"What? Now?" I wasn't going to allow another defector. I just wasn't.

Dante tugged on my ponytail. "I wouldn't have contributed much. The students are looking to you to lead them. But I'll be back." His words were light, but the way he crushed me to his chest in a bear hug showed just how worried he was.

I wrapped my arms around his middle. "You need to be careful, too. I couldn't stand it if anything happened to you guys."

"Don't worry about us, pet." Gareth rubbed my lower back and topped it off with a little ass-squeeze. "Look after yourself."

Dante stiffened then shot his hand out and grabbed Gareth's arm, jerking it from my body. He bared his fangs, the look he shot the demon both terrifying and somehow turning me on.

It was a strange combination.

"Whoa." I held my hands up. "I thought we'd gotten past this jealousy after..." After the two of them had fucked me senseless together. Yeah, that didn't roll off the tongue easily.

Dante felt one pointed incisor with his thumb, the color draining from his face. "Sorry. I didn't mean that to happen."

"You'd best get your vampire side under control, pup." Gareth hefted his bag. "And next time you touch me, you'll lose that arm."

The fangs that had started retreating dropped back down fully. Dante flew forward, swinging his fist.

Gareth's head whipped back from the impact, but the rest of his body remained immobile. Slowly, he swiveled his head forward, his eyes hard and flat and completely black. Three deep gashes crossed his cheek, dripping blood.

He dropped his bag. "Right."

I grabbed Dante's arm and yanked him away from the angry demon. Dante gave me no resistance. He was too busy staring at his red-tipped fingernails in horror.

I put a hand on Gareth's chest. "No. He didn't mean it. We can't hurt each other."

He lowered his chin. "Step aside."

"No." I put my weight into it and tried to push him back a step. Nothing moved but my feet, sliding against the mats. "You said yourself that he doesn't have control over it yet. It was an accident. And all of us need to stay healthy. We have a farkin' war ahead of us!"

Gareth stared at me a few moments longer. Then his pupils shrank, snapping back to normal, and I breathed a sigh of relief. He gave me a terse nod.

I patted my pockets then looked around but didn't see anything to staunch the bleeding on his cheek. I touched the skin above the first gouge, wincing. "Can you magic this closed?"

"It's fine." Gareth picked up his bag.

"Gareth..." Dante swallowed and looked away.

The demon ignored him. "I'll be back as soon as possible," he told me.

"But, your face." He couldn't just leave with blood dripping onto his T-shirt. Who did that? "Do either of you have a cloth?" No one said anything. "A handkerchief?" All I got were two blank gazes. Sheesh, when did men stop carrying handkerchiefs? "Well, let me get some gauze and clean it—"

"It's fine," Gareth repeated. Then, with one last look at me, he turned and blipped out of existence.

Demon apparition magic really was the bomb.

I rubbed at a knot in the back of my neck and turned to Dante. "Are you okay?" I hadn't really thought about it before. I'd been too freaked out that one of my lovers was a vamp and hadn't told me. But the fact that Dante sprouted fangs and claws when he got pissed was probably freaking the hell out of him. It couldn't be easy discovering a part of who you were was something you detested.

I'd had a hard enough time when I found out I was a witch. My recent werewolf bite hadn't changed me, but that full moon after the attack had been horrible. I'd felt sick all evening, waiting and wondering if I was going to sprout fur all of a sudden. But I'd had hope that I'd be okay. Dante didn't have that hope. "If you want—"

"I've gotta go." Dante turned on his heel and almost sprinted from the room.

"—to talk, I'd be happy to listen," I said to Gareth's empty gym. I planted my hands on my hips. Well, shit.

For someone who had more men than I knew what to do with, I could feel awfully abandoned at times.

At least Bane would be there for me at the gym. Most likely because he didn't trust me to lead an army, and to be fair, he was right about that. But he'd be there.

I turned and trudged out of Gareth's, heading for the school gym.

One thing I could always count on was Sinjin Bane, ready to take control and tell me what to do.

What did it say about my life that Bane's bossiness was the best thing I had going for me right now?

Chapter Five

"They're your army." Bane flicked a piece of lint from the sleeve of his tweed blazer. "You need to take the reins."

"No." I tapped my toe on the floor. This wasn't happening. Gareth was in hell, Dante ditched me, and now Bane wasn't being his usual bossy self? The gym was near bursting with students, some of them interested, others eager, but most of them probably just wanting to be entertained by whatever freakshow I was likely to put on. And Bane wanted me to mold them into something resembling a fighting squad?

My world tilted, and I had a moment of vertigo. "You like telling people what to do," I said. "This might have been my hare-brained idea, but you're the one who can execute it."

He huffed out a sigh. "You give yourself too little credit. The students will follow you, more so than they would their stuffy professor." He arched an eyebrow. "And, yes, I do know what is said about me."

"Then you must know that the entire female student body, and some of the guys, too, are hot for teacher." Which didn't make me happy, but who could blame them? Bane was yummy. I crossed my arms over my chest. "They'll follow you anywhere."

"Delaney..."

"Besides, do you really want *me* teaching them battle spells?" I pounded that nail in his coffin. "Didn't you once call me 'a powder keg of uncontrolled power, confusion, and recklessness?'"

His face blanched. "That was before, when you were still learning," he said weakly.

"That was two weeks ago."

He pressed his lips into a white slash. "Fine," he bit out. "I'll help train your recruits. But I still have white lodges to work with, research on the prophecy to do, spies to contact to find out who our enemy is—"

"Yeah, yeah, you're a busy guy, I get it." I waved my hand through the air. Now that I'd gotten my way, I could afford to be a bit flippant. I grinned. "Now go get these kids in fighting shape."

He gave me a look as he stalked past, one that dampened my panties and promised all sorts of retribution. If it had come from Gareth or Dante, I would have been excited. But since it came from Professor Nothing's-Going-to-Happen-Between-Us Bane, it just made me sad.

"All right, listen up." Bane's voice boomed through the gym. "The time for practicing your magic with training wheels on is over. I want you to form lines facing an opponent standing ten feet apart."

The students scrambled to do as he said, except for a small group off to the side. Hazel was whispering furiously at Ophelia. Quincy had his hand on Hazel's shoulder, looking like he was holding her back from flying at our nemesis.

I left Bane to it and hurried over to see what Ophelia had done now. "What's going on?" I asked my friends.

Unfortunately, it was Ophelia who responded. "This witch," she said, sneering, "thinks she can kick me out of the gym. It's a public space on the academy campus and I'm a paying student, unlike some people." She gave me a pointed look, like being here on scholarship made me less worthy to enjoy school facilities. "I'm staying."

"She's taking notes and reporting our activities back to her father," Hazel said through gritted teeth. She jabbed her finger at Ophelia. "If you aren't a part of the solution, get the hell out."

"Making sure you reprobates don't get us all killed is the solution." Ophelia cocked a hip. "I'm staying. Deal with it."

I darted in front of Hazel before she could draw blood. "It's okay. Let her watch. Maybe she'll learn something." I knew whatever Ophelia reported back to her dad wouldn't be flattering to me, but what else was new? I didn't have time for her petty BS.

Hazel raked her hand through her hair. "I just want to make sure you're safe before—"

"Before what?"

Her face flushed. She darted a glance at Quincy. He looked down at his feet. "Uh, before the war starts," she said. "You don't need any backstabbers around you." She glared over my shoulder.

I tilted my head, examining my friend. "Are you okay? You seem...weird."

Hazel's widow's peak dipped toward her eyebrows. "I like being weird."

"Yeah, but you seem like more of a freak show than usual," Ophelia put in. She narrowed her eyes, and if I didn't know her better, I would have sworn I saw a hint of concern on her face.

"It's... uh..." Hazel stared at her shoes. She sighed. "We need to tell you som—"

"Miss Jones!" Bane's voice bellowed across the gym. "Would you please come here?"

My shoulders rounded. I hadn't thought I'd be able to stay out of army-building for long, but I'd hoped for a couple more minutes. "We'll talk later," I told Hazel and Quincy and trotted toward Bane.

"Many of your fellow students are competent with the spells from your Combat & Defense class." He nodded approvingly at the crowd. "But it's time for them to learn a few basic combat spells that aren't scholastically approved by the council." The edges of his eyes crinkled and the corners of his mouth turned up. He looked like an angel thinking very naughty things.

My lower belly quivered, both from nerves and because one look from this man and I turned to jelly. Whatever he had planned wouldn't be fun for me. His smirk told me that. But he looked so damn good while plotting against me that I didn't care.

"I need a body to demonstrate the spells upon." His smirk grew into a full-fledged smile. "I've nominated you for the position."

I changed my mind. I cared. "Are you sure? I think one of the third year's would be better able—"

"I'm sure." He leaned close. "This was your idea."

"Yeah." And I was starting to regret it. What the hell did I know about war? I didn't even know anyone who'd been in the military. I should ask Hazel if she could find me a copy of that Art of War book by that ancient Chinese dude. It sounded like he knew what he was talking about.

"All right." I sulked away from him, finding one of the blue mats some students had spread on the floor. My ass was already feeling its future pain of bouncing off it, but at least I wouldn't be hitting the hardwood.

I turned and faced him. I took a deep breath. It was for the good of the world. I could take being zapped a couple times, though I didn't like that I wasn't even supposed to try to fight back.

"Hit me with your best shot."

Chapter Six

Dante

"Are you absolutely certain?" My heart twisted and I felt like I might throw up. This was going to devastate Delaney. Absolutely wreck her. She'd had a hard time accepting I was part vampire. Vamps were as sweet as baby lambs compared to Glauxo demons.

The four members of my white lodge nodded in unison. They sat in front of me, wearing identical light gray robes and solemn expressions. "The oracles agree with our information gathering," one said. "It was hidden well, but the truth will always out."

Another spoke. "This is a strike against her." They looked at each other significantly.

"It tells us nothing." I gritted my teeth. I knew what they were thinking. That in order to protect the lives of many, they might have to sacrifice hers.

I wouldn't let them. "As we speak she's training an army to fight against the evil that confronts us. She fights on our side. You need to trust me on this."

They were silent. I don't think they trusted me. I had, after all, only worked for them for a couple of years.

And I was in a relationship with the person in question.

My gums ached as my incisors prodded at them. The vampire in me wanted to bare my fangs, warn them of just how deadly the consequences would be if they went after Delaney. But revealing my true nature to the lodge would only put a mark on my back, too.

An elderly witch inclined her head. "We will wait. And watch."

It was the best I could hope for. Everyone's nerves were winding tighter and tighter, and I could smell the panic brewing in the air. I inclined my head and strode from the room.

I wondered who they would send for her. Which co-worker I'd have to kill to protect my love. I found an empty room and concentrated on my apartment back at the academy, building a portal.

Maybe it wouldn't be a lodge member. They might hire out for the wet work. They seemed to like letting others get dirty while they pretended to remain pristine.

Bane was one of their resources. He and the lodge traded information, and I knew he had assisted them in the past. And much as I wanted to believe he'd never hurt Delaney, there was something about the professor I just didn't trust.

I stepped through my portal into my bedroom...and right in front of another professor I didn't trust.

"Killough." I snarled. "What are you doing in my room?"

The vampire leaned forward on his perch on my sofa and rested his elbows on his knees. "Easy, friend. I've come to talk. To see how you are doing with your transition."

I stalked to my mini-fridge and pulled a bottle of water from it. "And you couldn't have done that by knocking on my door instead of breaking and entering?"

He lifted his hands, palms up. "Would you have answered?"

Hell, no. I twisted off the cap and sucked down some water, hoping to cool my anger.

Everything made me angry now that my fangs had dropped. The fact that I had fangs pissed me off. That I'd found a woman I wanted to be with and we had to worry about some asshole trying to destroy the world.

That Delaney let another asshole touch her.

That I enjoyed watching it. That uncomfortable fact really set my fangs on edge.

Christ, if Delaney hadn't stopped me, I would have ripped out Gareth's throat. Or tried to. And I'd always been the nice guy. The easy going one. I rubbed my temple. Entering into my vampire powers was like some hellish version of puberty.

And a vampire sat before me who had been through it before. If I was smart, I'd rein in my temper and learn from him.

I grabbed my desk chair, turned it around, and straddled it, facing Killough. I fiddled with the bottle cap, screwing and unscrewing it. "My control isn't what it should be."

He nodded. "That is always the case with our kind. But it will develop."

And we didn't have time for me to work through it on my own. Not when my lack of control could hurt someone I cared about. I knew this, but it still took every ounce of willpower for me to open my mouth and ask, “Will you help me? I need my vampire and warlock sides to work as one.”

Killough rolled to his feet. He flicked his long, blond ponytail over his shoulder. “I would be honored. When we are through, you will be a force to be reckoned with. Half mage. Half vampire. It is a powerful combination.”

I nodded, my shoulders sagging in relief. I should have gone to him earlier, the first time my anger had spiked and my fangs had dropped.

I could only hope later was better than never.

Chapter Seven

Delaney

I peeled off the lid to the five-gallon tub of ice cream, my spoon at the ready. A thick layer of freezer burn separated me from the rocky road. "Craptastic."

My voice soundly oddly loud in the deserted cafeteria. It was one in the morning, and everyone smart was already in bed.

Either that, or had fled home. Throughout the day, the student body numbers had dwindled, more and more students trickling out from our army training and quietly packing their belongings.

I couldn't blame them. Why should anyone believe that we faced a war? And even if they did believe me, they'd be crazy to follow me into battle.

But the attrition had hurt. If I was the farkin' Chosen One, I should be able to inspire an army and lead them, damn it. Add to that the hours of playing Bane's crash test dummy and all the resulting aches and bruises, and I really needed some ice cream.

I held my hand over the tub, gathered my intention to stuff my face sick, and felt my energy hum through me. The ice layer shimmered, then disappeared. "Ha!" I could control my magic for the important things. I just needed the right motivation: food.

I shoveled in a huge tablespoon full of chocolatey goodness. I'd only ever attempted the disappearing spell in class to clean up the bowl of ink I'd knocked over, but its usefulness knew no bounds.

My gut twisted. Could I use it to disappear an enemy? Just wave my hands and poof, my opponent was gone?

I shoved another spoonful in my mouth. It really sucked that I had to think about the martial application of everything now. To consider ways to kill.

"Delaney." Hazel trotted into the cafeteria, Quincy on her heels. "Thank Goddess we found you in time. I told you we should have looked here first," she said to Quincy.

He shrugged.

Hazel dumped her book bag on the floor and dropped into a seat across from me, Quincy at her side. She placed her palms flat on the table. "This isn't easy to say but I don't have time to soft pedal it." She stared me straight in the eyes. "Quincy and I are leaving. Our parents are insisting that we come home. They don't think it's safe here."

My spoon slipped from my fingers, landing in the ice cream. "Wait. What? You're leaving?"

Hazel nodded, looking a bit green. In a rare show of physical affection, Quincy reached across the table and squeezed my hand.

"We're so sorry, Delaney." Hazel pushed her hair behind her ear. "We argued with them for hours, but..."

"They're your parents." I swallowed, tasting bile. And most people had parents they listened to and respected. "I understand. In fact, I even agree. I don't want to see you guys in danger, either." It would suck not having them by my side during the upcoming battle, but it was also a relief. I wouldn't have to worry about being responsible if they got injured. Or dead.

"Come with us." Quincy's voice was always a surprise, and I jerked my gaze to his. His face was dead serious and looking much older than his nineteen years. "You can hide at my house. Stay out of it."

"I..." God, it was tempting. Moving in with a normal family. Having a mom and dad figure cooking for us, looking after us. But it was a dream. "I can't. My place is here." Fighting with Gareth, Bane, and Dante. "Besides, I would only bring the danger to you. They won't stop coming after me. They think I'm a threat." Whoever 'they' were.

"Remember what Hedwig said." Hazel pulled the ice cream tub in front of her and picked up my spoon. "You make your own destiny. You don't have to fight."

"If the bad guys would leave me alone maybe you'd be right." Could I do it? Could I just walk away and turn my back when the war between the magical people broke out? Maybe. The fact that I could even consider such a thing didn't make me proud, but there it was. After all, I'd only been a witch for a couple of months. Most of my life had been spent in the human world.

But it wasn't a decision I had to concern myself about. Someone thought I was the Chosen One, the witch who would stop him from implementing his plan. No matter where I went to hide, he'd come after me.

I watched Hazel eat my ice cream, and smiled. I must really love her if her dessert-stealing habit didn't tick me off. "I hope when this is all over we can, I don't know, hang out? Go out for coffee?" What did witches do for fun?

I bit my lip. It was like leaving high school all over again. My friends and I told each other we'd still see each other, but in the back of my mind I'd known it would never happen. They'd had dances to go to, tests to study for, boys to flirt with. My life had been different. We'd been traveling down two separate paths, and the phone calls and texts had dwindled to nothing.

Quincy rolled his eyes. Hazel snorted. "Bitch, before this is over we're going to be sneaking out to see you. I've been practicing creating portals, and Quince said he'll be my guinea pig."

Our friend looked a little green at that, but he nodded stoutly.

"We'll be talking to you so much you're going to stop answering our calls," Hazel continued. "And when this is over, well..." She stabbed the spoon into the tub, sighing. "Do you think the academy will reopen? It would have been nice to have a degree from Raven."

"I don't know." The idea of resuming classes as usual was too surreal to contemplate. I'd enjoyed my time here, but if we survived a global war, coming back and becoming a student again just seemed weird.

"When are you guys leaving?" I asked.

"Now." Hazel scratched at a mark on the table. "Our parents are waiting for us outside."

We all remained silent as I digested that bit of crap news. It felt like my security blanket was being torn away. I just wanted a couple more minutes to cuddle with it.

"I almost forgot." Hazel pushed the ice cream away and dug through her bag. She pulled out two books. "I found Sun Tzu's *The Art of War* as you asked, and also..." She placed a second book on top of the first, spinning it around so I could read the cover. The edges were worn and the pages looked a bit warped like they'd gotten wet, but I recognized the title. It had been plastered over Instagram a year or two back, one of those books that it seemed like everyone was reading.

Except of course I hadn't.

"This is my go-to book when I'm in a mood," Hazel said. "I can't even count how many times I've read it. It's amazing. I want you to have it."

"It looks like this book means a lot to you." I nudged it back in her direction. "You keep it."

Hazel huffed. "I know you're not big on reading, but trust me. You'll love it."

I examined the spine. It was at least three times as thick as *The Art of War*. My brain hurt just thinking about reading all that. "I'll wait for it to be made into a movie."

Hazel pushed it back at me, and I had to grab it before it toppled into my lap. "Trust me," she repeated. "When things are getting rough and you're pissed off at one of your guys—"

I sucked in a sharp breath.

"—and yes, we know about that, you naughty slut." She smirked. "But when you're feeling like crap, start reading this book. I swear it's better than a therapist."

I gathered the books to my chest. I didn't know if I'd read it, if I'd have time even, but it obviously meant a lot to Hazel. So it meant a lot to me.

"I will," I told her. Maybe I'd start reading it tonight. Gareth was incommunicado in hell, my 'army' was looking more like a sad pep rally, and now my besties were abandoning me. I couldn't feel much crappier.

"Now introduce me to your parents." I stood, forcing a smile. "I want to meet the witches who begat you two hell-demons."

Chapter Eight

I'd been wrong. I really could feel crappier.

"Tell me you're kidding." I looked from Dante to Bane and back again. I wheezed quietly, my lungs not wanting to fill with air.

Dante stepped close and placed his hand on my shoulder, squeezing. "I'm sorry, Delaney. I know this must be hard—"

"Hard?" I shrugged his hand off and paced across Bane's living room. I needed to move. Go for a run. Punch something. They couldn't be right. There was no way it was possible.

"It checks out," Bane said. "When Rider's white lodge contacted me, I spoke with my own sources. It explains a lot."

A hysterical laugh burbled out of me. "Does it? My dad being a... a..." I couldn't even say the word. I slashed my hand through the air. "Does it explain why I'm the Chosen One? How it's possible I might decide to destroy the world?"

Jesus, it did explain it. I clutched my stomach, willing the nausea away. It explained everything. If only I could wrap my head around my lazy, a-hole of a father being a...

"Being part demon doesn't mean you're evil." Dante grabbed both my shoulders and pinned me with his gaze. "Just look at Gareth."

Right. Gareth. He was all demon and he was a good guy. But... "What kind of demon did you say my dad was? Glauxo? Isn't that kind one of the worst of the worst?" Because of Gareth, I'd listened well to the section of my History of Magic class when we'd discussed demons. Glauxo demons had been near the top of my list of creatures I didn't want to meet.

Dante and Bane exchanged uneasy glances.

Bane cleared his throat. "They have their faults."

Dante cupped the back of my neck. “Vamps have their flaws, too.” He tapped his incisor. “But it doesn’t define me.” He blinked. “Who my father is *doesn’t* define me. And your dad’s lineage doesn’t define you, either.” He gave me his patented panty-melting smile that warmed every part of me. “We’re both mutts. We decide who we’re going to be.”

My body leaned into him. It couldn’t help it. I was caught in his gravity. “Calling your girl a dog isn’t the best way to ensure some nookie,” I joked. Then blushed. “Not that I’m saying I’m your girl.” I flicked a guilty glance at Bane. “I mean, not that I’m not saying that but...” My face flamed hotter. Why couldn’t I talk? Who were those women who said the right thing at the right time? And why couldn’t I be them?

Dante tightened his grip on me. “You’re my girl. Even if—” He scowled at Bane.

Even if I wanted Bane, too. Even when I was also Gareth’s.

I rubbed my forehead. You’d think facing war and death would give a girl a little clarity.

Bane exhaled sharply. “This isn’t the time to worry about Miss Jones’s relationship status.” He glared at the points where Dante touched me, his own hands clenching and unclenching. “And while this new information is interesting, I don't know that it actually helps us."

"Except to give you a good reason why I might choose evil." I stepped away from Dante, not wanting his comfort. Not when it felt like a lie. "If I was just witch and human, most people wouldn't worry about me going to the dark side." I wouldn't worry about me going evil. I swallowed. But with something unknown inside me...

Had that been my demon side that had clawed out when Bane had tried to strip my powers? Because that bitch was capable of anything. "Be honest. How many people on our side think I'll end the magical world? That I won't be the savior, but the destroyer?"

Dante protested, but I kept my gaze on Bane. Dante led with his heart; I knew he'd stand by me no matter what.

Bane was a creature of intellect. And deep morals. He'd do what he thought was right, even if it cost him, and me.

The edges of his eyes tightened, the motion gone so quickly I almost missed it. "We looked for you because we thought you'd save us. Nothing has changed."

"Bane." My voice was a low warning. I was tired of the protective bullshit. "Tell me the truth."

His Adam's apple bobbed. "The truth is you're very powerful and we need you on our side."

Still a deflection. "Bane!"

His muscles sagged, his shoulders slumping. It was like watching a tire deflate. "We don't know, Delaney. *I* don't know. I know you *want* to save the world, that your heart is in the right place, but..."

"But shit happens." And in the magical world, shit happened fast. One day I could be training to fight the big bad, the next day I might be his lap monkey. Crap on a cracker, maybe I could even be spelled into doing the wrong thing. Into betraying my friends.

I rubbed at the headache forming above my eye. "And if that happens?"

"If that happens—" He bit off his words, his jaw hardening. "If that happens, I'll take care of it."

Meaning he'd take care of me. Black dots danced in front of my eyes. Meaning he'd kill me.

A part of me was torn open. How could he even think of hurting me when I'd fucking die for him? But another part of me was relieved. Because it didn't fully trust that I'd do the right thing, either. Not when half of me was demon. And it wanted reassurance that someone I trusted would put me down if necessary.

"What the fuck does that mean?" Dante growled. He took a step toward Bane. "If you think—"

I grabbed his arm, as much to hold him back as to keep myself upright. My lungs still weren't functioning right and my legs wanted nothing more than to collapse so I could curl up on the floor and pretend this wasn't happening. "Don't," I managed to squeak out, shaking my head. "He's right. It would be the right thing to do."

Dante scowled. "Bullshit." But he dragged me into his arms and held me like I was everything to him, and that was nice. "This isn't over," he told Bane.

I clung to him, breathing in his soap and warm skin, and ignored their silent argument. Because although I couldn't see it, I could feel their hot glares and I knew words would be had later.

But that wasn't my concern at the moment. I took one more deep breath, soaking up Dante's strength and hoping it would transfer to me, before stepping back and giving my guys my best smile.

I could tell from their expressions it was shaky as hell.

I firmed it up and planted my hands on my hips. "Well, who wants to come with me to see dear, old pops?"

Chapter Nine

My dad scratched his stomach, his fingertips getting lost in his belly hair. He reached for his beer, his gaze never leaving the huge, flat-screen TV perched on top of a dresser.

My skin flared hot then cold. Hot then cold. It was like I was a damn water faucet switching back and forth. My body didn't know whether to shrivel up in embarrassment that Dante and Bane were here, in my old home, meeting the person who'd given me half his DNA, or to fly into a rage that after not seeing his daughter in four years and three months, he was more interested in Jerry Springer reruns than in talking to me.

I guess I was a hypocrite, though, cause I sure as shit didn't want to catch up with him, either. If I didn't have to be here, I wouldn't.

My gaze was dragged to the kitchen wall. To the painted cutting board hanging from a nail. My mom had bought it, I knew, even though I didn't remember it, on a family trip to Pennsylvania. It was narrower than most cutting boards, with a handle and decorated with hex signs.

A shiver wracked my body.

Dante leaned into me, draping his arm over the back of the sofa we sat on and resting his hand on my shoulder. Bane sat on my other side, his thigh warm against mine. Nothing bad could happen with these two men by my sides.

My burgeoning panic eased. I even managed to make my voice light. "So, Dad, a demon, huh? Don't you think that's something you should have told me?"

He grunted and turned the volume up on the TV with his remote. "Why bother? You're a half-breed. It's not like I have to worry about you having Glauxo strength."

The remote was ripped from his hands. It hovered in the air in front of Bane. The TV blinked off and the remote caved in on itself, the metal and plastic bending and folding until only a tiny ball was left. Bane let it drop to the ground.

"You son of a bitch." My dad placed his hands on the armrests of his chair and started to heave his bulk up.

Bane raised a hand, and my dad froze. "Shane, let's not do this today, hmm?" His English accent sounded extra crisp. "We've come with your daughter for a twenty-minute discussion. You will give her your full attention for that time." He waved a finger, and my dad was jerked back into his chair.

My dad made a rumbling sound deep in his chest.

I blinked and looked closer. Nope, his eyes were the same dark blue color they always were. I must have imagined the red.

"Why are you living like a human?" I knew Dante wanted to ease the tension in the room, but there was genuine curiosity in his voice, too. "You're a demon, you were married to a witch. Why not live in the magical world?"

My dad settled back in his chair. He shrugged. "I like playing a human. Good food. Good TV. No asshole warlocks harassing me." He gave Bane a pointed look. "Besides, her mom wanted kids. I never did. But she was scared."

"The prophecy," Bane said.

My dad nodded. "Cat was born the year of the prophecy. She always worried she'd give birth to the Chosen One. So we decided to live as humans. Keep any prying eyes off the brat in case anyone suspected she was the one." He snorted. "If she'd lived longer, she would have seen there was nothing to worry about. Such a useless child could never be the one to save the world."

My intestines twisted, twirling around each other like slippery eels. I controlled the urge to vomit. "I guess the joke's on you." I locked eyes with my father. "Surprise, Dad. You're looking at the Chosen One."

He laughed, like I'd told a good joke. When no one else joined in, his chuckles drifted off. "Get the fuck outta here."

Dante stiffened beside me. "She's your daughter. Treat her with respect."

My dad rolled his eyes. "Excuse my surprise." His gaze flicked to the wall. To the cutting board. "I didn't think the world's savior would be someone who whined so much as a child."

A low hum started, growing louder. I thought it was in my head, my own humiliation and anger screwing with me, until I saw the walls vibrating.

My dad looked around, worry battling with annoyance on his face.

I rested my hand on Bane's thigh. The humming quieted.

He knew. Somehow Bane knew what my dad had done to me. I'd never wanted anyone to know. Had never told anyone, not even my friends. There were too many raw emotions wrapped up in being your dad's punching bag. Fear, disgust, humiliation, fear, hatred, fucked-up guilt, and oh yeah, did I mention fear?

Learning to fight had saved my life in more ways than one. Learning how to take a punch, to give back as good as I was getting, had calmed something in me that was raging to explode.

I squeezed Bane's leg. And him knowing about all that? Well, that thought didn't scare me the way it used to.

"You're greedy, brutish, lazy, and vengeful," Bane said. "The hallmark characteristics of a Glauxo demon. It makes perfect sense why you'd live as a human."

"Hey!" Okay, I wasn't actually a human, but until a couple of months ago, I'd thought I'd been one. And there were lots of good ones out there. "Just because my dad's a jerk doesn't mean you should be a human-bigot. A human invented donuts. They'll have my everlasting love and gratitude."

The corners of Bane's lips twitched. "Are you sure it was a human?"

I frowned. No, I wasn't sure, It could have been a witch. I blinked. Did witches have a culinary tradition? This could change everything.

My dad belched and reached for his beer. "I always could bribe you with food when you were little. You'd shut up for chocolate."

My shoulder blades drew back. No need for him to know I still did. "Well, this has been fun. I was hoping you'd be able to tell me something more about the prophecy, but I can see that was a stupid idea. I hope I won't see you on the battlefield fighting for the other side."

He flapped his hand. "Fighting takes more energy than most Glauxos want to expend. You won't have to worry about our kind." He pursed his lips. "Probably."

I stood, Bane and Dante following. "Thanks." For nothing. He didn't even care his daughter would be fighting for her life soon. Lead settled in my belly. If I had half his DNA weighing me down, my odds for success didn't look so bright anymore.

Not that they'd ever been great.

Fuck me, I was going to die.

He got up and shuffled to the TV, turning it on manually. "If you want to stay out of it, you could always strip your powers. Then you'd be no use to either side in a fight."

My hand clenched. A part of me wanted to turn my magic on him, blast him into the wall.

Another part of me was tempted.

"I tried a spell to bind her powers." Bane crossed his arms over his chest. "It didn't go well."

My dad barked out a laugh. He found a new channel on the TV and strolled back to his chair, settling in. "Spells. That would be useless. Someone else could do another spell to bring her powers back. No, what you'd need is the Root."

"The Root? The Root of Corruption? That's a myth." Dante mirrored Bane's stance, unintentionally I was sure. But they were like my two tough-ass bookends. I almost smiled. I would have if I'd known what the heck they were talking about.

"Is it?" My dad crushed his beer can and another one appeared on the table next to him. So he did use some magic.

"The only eye-witness accounts of its existence are over three thousand years old," Bane said. He rubbed his jaw. "If it's real, it's been hidden well."

"What is the Root of Corruption?"

Bane narrowed his eyes, staring into space. "It's said to be a chalice—"

"Or bowl," Dante interjected. "I've read the mythology where it describes it as a bowl."

"Details get lost in translation," Bane agreed. "It's said if you drink your opponent's blood from it, you strip them of their powers."

"And take them into yourself." Her dad licked his bottom lip. "Don't forget that part. It would bring a pretty penny, that's for sure. But it's guarded by traps. Any profit wasn't worth the risk."

"You're saying you know where it is?" Dante blinked in disbelief.

"I might." Her dad shifted. "What's it worth to you?"

Bane, Dante, and I looked at each other. I shrugged. I wasn't looking to strip my powers, but it seemed like a neat toy. A tool that might come in handy. If it existed.

Dante drew his lips back, his fangs dropping. In a flash, he was by my dad's side, hand wrapped around his throat. "What's it worth to you not to have your throat ripped out?"

My dad paled, and it took me a second to remember. He hated vampires, or at least the vampire movies that

I'd wanted to see as a kid. He'd lost his shit when he'd caught me watching *The Lost Boys*.

Now, faced with a real vamp, he didn't look happy. "In the In-Between. Prepare to be tested. Many demons have tried to recover it. None have survived."

Dante patted his chest. He retracted his fangs. "Good boy. You get to live to see another day."

My father clenched his fists, his face turning red. For just a fraction of a second, it wasn't my dad sitting in his lounge chair. Not my human dad, anyway. A hideous troll-like demon sat there, its skin gray as death, eyes glowing red.

I stepped back in horror. Was that what was inside me? Just as quickly, the vision was gone. Just my normal, asshole dad again.

Okay. I took a deep breath. Instead of focusing on the fact that I had *that* inside me and if any of my guys saw it they'd never want to sleep with me again, I looked at the positive. I was part monster. A bad ass. And I didn't have to take his shit ever again.

I didn't think about it, my magic flowing instinctively. Raising my hand, I pulled the cutting board off the wall with my energy and smashed it to the ground. It took three strikes before the fucking board split into pieces.

It could never hurt me again. My dad could never hurt me again.

I had a war in front of me. Death was a strong possibility. But I felt free. Light, like weights had been lifted from my shoulders.

I'd run away from my dad four years ago, but today I finally felt liberated.

"Bye, Dad." I turned on my heel and left his dump of an apartment. I never had to set foot in there again.

Dante caught up with me when I hit the sidewalk. "You okay?"

I nodded. "Yeah." Except I was part Glauxo demon. But that wasn't something I could discuss with him. He had enough problems dealing with being half vampire.

Bane joined us. "And I thought Gareth had daddy issues."

I gave him a small smile. The stodgy professor was trying to cheer me up. His joke didn't land home, but the intent behind it warmed me straight through. "Well, I guess we know where my inner bitch comes from."

Bane turned me to face him, squeezing my arms. "You are nothing like your father. Nothing."

What was it Bane had said? Glauxo demons were known for being greedy, brutish, lazy, and vengeful?

That wasn't a perfect description of me, but it wasn't completely wrong, either.

My heart clenched. I was definitely greedy. I wanted three men; settling for one left me feeling incomplete. Brutish? I liked to fight with my hands, making Bane despair of my ever excelling with magic. And as much as I liked training, I loved plunking my ass on the sofa and vegging out in front of the TV watching Netflix and eating ice cream.

And vengeful? The witch inside me growled. Yeah, if we hadn't found Bane alive and well, something told me my inner bitch wouldn't have taken it well. That I might have even gone nuclear. There would have been blood.

But my future wasn't going to be filled with tea parties. I was going into battle. Perhaps vengeance and brutality were what I needed to win.

I might not like it that I was half-demon, but I could use it to my advantage.

I linked my arms through theirs and headed for the nearest alley. "Come on. One of you create a portal and get us the hell out of here."

Chapter Ten

"Great job, Jezamine!" I shouted encouragement as the witch stunned her opponent. The group in the gym was smaller than that first day when Bane had trained my 'army,' but it was a good group. Full of strong and determined witches and warlocks. Ones who believed a war was coming and wanted to fight on the right side.

What it lacked in numbers (we only had twenty-eight student-fighters) it made up for in grit. All it lacked were Hazel and Quincy.

I rubbed my breastbone. Every day I looked for them in the group before I remembered they were gone. We Facetimed, but it wasn't the same.

A bolt of green energy flew toward my head, and I shot my hands up to redirect it. "Your aim's a little off there, Xerxes. Look to where your target is, not at your hands when launching your spell."

He nodded, his cheeks growing pink, but got back in a sparring position with his partner.

Bane strolled to my side, his hands in his slack's pockets. "They're looking better."

I nodded. It was amazing what four days of non-stop training would do. Really, the modern education system needed work. Instead of trapping students in classrooms, teachers should make education more practical. But that was just my two cents.

Bane handed me a granola bar, and I accepted it gratefully. The kitchens had been stocked with ready-to-eat meals as no one was left to cook the good stuff, and I'd come to live off of the granola bars and fruit Bane brought me while we trained.

I crunched down on the oat and honey concoction. It was okay and definitely served its purpose, but it was no bourbon pecan waffles or chicken Kiev. I sighed. Perhaps the cook leaving was for the best. My jeans had been getting a bit tight, and I didn't want to go into battle with sugar weight slowing me down.

But after the war was over, I was binging on three dozen jelly donuts.

"I heard from Gareth," Bane said.

"What?" I spun, the training forgotten. "What did he say? Why did he contact you and not me? Is he coming back soon?"

"He said little, being as loquacious as ever, beyond that he is unharmed and doesn't know when he can leave." He brushed a swath of dark hair out of his eyes. "And I assume he wants to limit contact with you just in case there is someone watching who doesn't know who you are. Unlikely as that may be."

"Hmmm." I turned back to the training session, crossing my arms over my chest. I appreciated the protectiveness, but he was the one in immediate danger. I needed to assure myself he was okay. Plus, I just wanted to talk to my demon, especially now that I'd discovered I was part demon. I had *questions*, and Gareth might be able to help me sort it all out.

"We discussed what your father said about the Root." Bane spit out the word 'father' like it pained him to say it. "Gareth and Mr. Rider have an idea about retrieving it."

I frowned. Gareth was talking to Dante, too, but not me. It was enough to give a girl a complex. "Planning on letting me in on the idea?"

"Of course." A line creased the skin between Bane's eyebrows. "Did you think we wouldn't?"

If they thought keeping me in the dark kept me safe? Maybe. But I didn't have time to debate the point. A flash of turquoise silk caught my eye. "Excuse me," I told Bane and marched across the gym to the girl trying to hide behind a large third year.

"What are you doing here?" I asked Ophelia. "You don't need to spy. I'm very open with what we're doing."

Ophelia tugged at the cuff to her colorful blouse. "I'm not spying on you. You're not that interesting."

"Yet here you are." I spread my arms wide, encompassing the whole gym. "If not to spy, then why be here?"

"Eykamthep," she muttered between gritted teeth.

I wrinkled my nose. "What?"

"Eykamtohelp," she said a little louder.

I cupped a hand to my ear. "Still not getting it."

Ophelia huffed. "I said, I came to help. Happy now?" She glared at me.

I rocked back on my heels. "Help how? By giving these guys a laugh when you try to humiliate me?" Which actually wasn't a bad idea. Not the me being humiliated part, but the laughing. These students had been training to exhaustion for several days now. A bit of comedy wouldn't hurt.

Ophelia shoved her hands in the pockets of her skinny jeans. "Look. I heard my parents talking about this war and prophecy business. You might not be as completely full of shit as I thought." She swallowed, looking vulnerable for a fraction of a second before her hard mask dropped back on her face. "I don't want my world to be destroyed. I can help."

I arched an eyebrow. "Hmmm."

Crap. I was starting to sound as pretentious as Bane with all my 'hmm-ing.' And I don't think I pulled it off as well as the sexy Brit.

Ophelia cocked her hip. "Look, do you want my help or not? You know I'm a good witch."

I blew out a breath. She was right. Annoying as she was, she was one of the top witches at Raven. And if she wasn't using this as an excuse to screw me over, she would be useful.

I gave a short nod. "You can train with Grimaldo." I smiled at the talented third year student. "Grim, don't go easy on her."

"Sure." He shrugged on a hoodie with the Death Star printed across the chest. "But not till tomorrow. It's five o'clock. A group of us are going to the Quarter to get dinner."

"Sounds like fun." Ophelia linked her arm through Grimaldo's, ignoring his raised eyebrows, and waggled her fingers at me. "Toodles, loser. See you tomorrow."

The students filed out of the gym, some talking in low voices, others laughing together. No one glanced back at me or invited me to their dinner plans.

I stomped to a bench and the bottle of water I'd left on it. Whoever said it was lonely at the top knew what he or she was talking about.

It was probably for the best. One, I didn't have money to eat out in New Orleans. And two... Well, two was hard to think about. I could be ordering these people to their deaths soon. Getting too familiar with them wouldn't help the cause.

But it just made me miss Hazel and Quincy more.

"Where do you think you're going?" Bane stood by the door, leaning casually on the handle of a battle axe like it was a cane.

My axe.

"You raiding Gareth's weapons stash?" I scooted to his side and took the axe, examining the double blades for any scratches. I rubbed out a smudge with the hem of my tank top.

"I merely thought we could do some after-hours training." He strolled to the middle of the gym. "I know you like fighting like a human, using metal and your fists as weapons, but I think we can meld your magic with your desire for mayhem."

I'd tried mixing up my spells with my physical strikes. Distract someone with the feeling of burning feet then follow that up by slicing off a tentacle. I thought it had been going fairly well, Bane's disdain for my human fighting style notwithstanding. "Well—"

The axe was ripped from my hands. It spun end over end, the metal blade glinting in the waning sunlight, right into Bane's outstretched hand.

"Hey!" I narrowed my eyes. Bane's magic twirled the weapon above his open hand in a fancy figure-eight pattern. "My axe." My words didn't have much heat. I was too intrigued with the possibility of using my magic to control the axe. Why the heck hadn't I thought of that?

He grinned. He curled the fingers of his upraised hand in a 'come get me' gesture. "You want it? Come take it."

Chapter Eleven

I ached down to my very bones. It had been two weeks of non-stop training. The student army was looking pretty good, if I did say so myself, and I was even impressed with my own new skills. But I didn't know how much longer we could continue at our grueling pace.

I stumbled over the edge of the carpet as I trudged to my room, smacking my hand against the hallway wall to stop my faceplant.

Two weeks of exhausting training.

Two weeks of hearing nothing from Gareth, except an 'I'm okay' transmitted through Bane or Dante.

I clenched and released my hands. Two weeks of waiting for another attack. For the next shoe to drop. I was almost disappointed when I went to bed at night and nothing had tried to kill me during the day. The tension was killing me.

There was a Big Bad out there. I could feel him amassing his power. Could hear the tension rising in the chatter of the witches around me. Their fear of the unknown growing. Even the most stalwart students were getting suspicious that there was actually a war on the horizon.

But nothing farkin' happened. I didn't particularly care for people trying to end my life, but I could really use an opponent's face to smash right about now.

I turned down the next corridor and bumped into a firm chest.

"Dante." The knots in my shoulders began to unravel. I'd seen him that morning at breakfast, such as it was, but he kept slipping out of the gym during drills. "Want to grab some popcorn and watch a movie?" Hopefully in his room with its ginormous feather-soft bed. I probably wouldn't stay awake more than five minutes into the movie, but snoozing on that bed in Dante's arms seemed like the best idea I'd had all day.

"I can't." He blinked rapidly. "I, uh, have to go meet someone. Uh, white lodge business."

I narrowed my eyes. "White lodge business, huh?" I didn't buy it. And I thought we were past the point of lying to each other.

But there must have still been some trust issues between us because instead of calling him on his BS, I shrugged and rolled onto my toes to peck his cheek. "Okay. Have fun with that. I'll see you tomorrow." I strolled away.

And turned right around when he disappeared down the next hallway.

Going into stealth mode, I tiptoed after the lying bastard. We snuck down to the main floor, across the great room and into the left wing of the academy. I thought for sure I'd be caught when I swallowed my spit the wrong way and had to bury my face in my arms to smother my coughing fit, but Dante didn't pause, just turned one more corner and entered a classroom.

When I could breathe again, (and how the hell does a person choke on her own saliva? It just didn't seem like that should be possible), I crept after him and pressed my ear to the door.

I didn't hear anything. It was my old Cryptozoology classroom, and it had been larger than most of the other rooms. To make room for the magical creatures Professor Paca brought in to show us, it had to be. If Dante was on the far side of the room, that could be why I didn't hear him.

Or maybe he was doing something that didn't require talking.

Meditation?

Yoga?

Neither of those seemed probable. And if Dante wanted to pretzel his body into interesting shapes, he could have been doing it in a more enjoyable manner with me.

I sucked in a breath and eased the door open an inch, plastering my eye to the gap.

And almost choked on my spit again.

Dante was down in the wide area made for magical creatures. It was built like a mini arena, with a low wooden fence ringing it. He hovered two feet from the ground in front of an equally buoyant Professor Killough. The vamp and half-vamp floated around each other, like two freaky opponents in a boxing ring, before Dante dipped his shoulders and flew at Killough.

The vampire's movements were a blur to my eye, but the end result was he remained hovering above the dirt floor and Dante lay sprawled face-down on it.

"You still think too much in terms of human movement." Killough drifted down until his feet touched the ground. He tossed his ponytail over his shoulder. "Vampires think of where they want to go, not all the steps needed to get there. Once you abandon the idea of needing to put one leg in front of the other to walk and just focus on the destination, you will be able to move faster than you've ever thought possible."

I squeezed through the opening in the door, slowly closed it, and pressed my back to the wall. The room was dark except for the lights above the mini arena so they shouldn't be able to see me, but I tried not to move nonetheless.

Dante picked himself up and dusted dirt from his T-shirt. "I get what you're saying. It's like driving. You don't look at the road right in front of you but where you want to go." He ran his hand up the back of his head. "But understanding what you're saying and implementing it are two different things."

"Indeed." Killough inclined his head.

One second the vampire was down in the ring, the next he was pressed to my side, his fingers trailing through my hair. "I've never driven a car," he said. His tone was friendly, like we'd been in the middle of a conversation, and not like he'd almost made me piss my pants. "Perhaps you could help explain the phenomenon Mr. Rider speaks of."

Dante spun to face us. His shoulders inched toward his ears. "Get away from her."

Killough ignored him. Even in the dim light, I could see his ice-blue eyes glinting with humor. Or was it hunger? I knew every girl at Raven would drop their panties for the beautiful vamp in a nano-second, but he filled me with nothing but uneasiness. Even knowing how amazing a vampire's bite could feel, I didn't want his teeth anywhere near my neck.

Only Dante was allowed to bite me.

Killough twirled a strand of my hair around his index finger, tugging at my scalp. "Instead of observing, perhaps Ms. Jones can make herself useful." He leaned in close to my head and inhaled. "We can—"

Killough's words were cut off by Dante's hand around his throat. Displaced air wafted across me and ebbed before I saw Dante standing next to me.

I shook my head. Blinked. One second he'd been in the ring, the next choking our professor. Moving just like Killough had told him to.

I tugged on Dante's arm. "Let him go. It was a teaching tactic." I looked at Killough. "Right?"

"Indeed." His lips twitched. "That demonstration helped with your speed problem, but sadly not your mental acuity. Do I need to remind you again that choking a vampire has no effect? We don't need air to survive."

Dante released him, flexing his hand. "Sorry. Just...don't touch her."

I placed my hand on his lower back and leaned into him. I liked it a little too much that this man was willing to throw down for me.

Killough smoothed the collar of his shirt. "Unfortunately, the demonstration didn't help your control issues. You're still letting your vampire side rule your emotions." He gave me a speculative look. "Perhaps when it comes to Ms. Jones, however, your knee-jerk reactions can be understood."

The vampire gave me a half-bow. "I apologize, Ms. Jones, but the little act was necessary to improve Mr. Rider's skills."

"I understand." I shifted my weight. And frankly, Dante's knee-jerk reaction had been hot as hell. "Are you guys going to fight some more?" Watching two sexy, supernaturally strong men going at it wasn't a horrible way to spend an evening.

Dante blew out a breath. "Yeah. I've gotten better integrating my vampire side with my warlock, but I need more practice if I'm going to be of any use in the war."

"That's not true," I argued. His warlock side was plenty powerful.

"What are you doing here?" he asked me. "Did you follow me?"

"Yeah." I worried my bottom lip. Should I feel ashamed for that? No, I really didn't think I should. "I wanted to see what you were up to. I knew you were lying about the lodge."

He dropped his head. "Sorry about that. I know we said we wouldn't lie to each other anymore, but it was only a small, white one. I just didn't want you to worry that I wouldn't be strong enough to protect you when the time came. I want to be the best. For you."

Awww. My chest warmed. This one always knew just what to say.

Then Killough had to go ruin our warm and fuzzy moment. "Ms. Jones followed you without your knowledge?" He tutted. "You should have been able to hear her. Instead of focusing on fighting and control, next lesson we train on utilizing your increased senses."

"Great," Dante muttered. "Something else I suck at."

I slapped his chest. "You don't suck." Well, not unless I asked him to. "Hey, do you mind an audience?" I jutted my chin at one of the chairs set close to the ring.

"Not if you don't mind seeing me get my ass kicked." The edges of Dante's eyes crinkled.

I sauntered to the chair and dropped into it. "Well, I prefer to be the one doing the ass-kicking, but this will work, too."

And it did, at least for me. When Dante and Killough squared off, a decided tingle hummed low in my belly. Sometimes the action was too fast for me to make out, but after each round, Dante stood there, chest heaving, getting sweatier and sweatier.

Killough didn't sweat, but he did take off his shirt when Dante did so the fabric wouldn't get torn.

My mouth went dry. Okay, the professor wasn't my cup of tea, but watching his chiseled body wrestling with Dante's, their muscles clenching, growls slipping from their mouths, well, it did things to me.

Naughty, yummy things.

It could only have been better if Dante had been sparring with Gareth or Bane.

Killough flew at Dante's feet, trying to take out his base.

Dante brought his elbow down on the vampire's back, the power behind it making me teeth rattle from ten feet away. Killough flipped, feet over head, and landed a cross on Dante's jaw, knocking him across the room.

Dante stopped his momentum seconds before he hit the ground, hovering inches from the dirt.

"Good job." Killough straightened. He strolled to the low fence and plucked his shirt from it, slipping it on. "I think that's enough for tonight."

"Are you sure?" My shoulders dropped as Dante pulled on his T-shirt. Too much lovely skin was being covered up. "I mean, we are facing the possible end of the world."

Killough's lips twitched. "I'm afraid so. But you're welcome to join us any night, assuming Mr. Rider has no objections." He slid the last button through its hole and smoothed the fabric. "As for me, I have a date with my lovely partner. If you two will excuse me." And without waiting for an answer, he slipped from the room.

"I wonder who he's dating."

Dante pulled me to my feet. "Do you care?"

I shrugged. "Just curious. There's going to be a lot of broken hearts among the female students."

"The only heart I care about is yours." He brushed his lips against mine, setting that heart to racing. And not just from his kiss. He was treading into dangerous territory. Touchy-feely territory. He wrapped his arms around my back. "I love you, Delaney."

Yep, dangerous territory indeed. My blood rushed through my ears, making me dizzy. The L-word. How the hell did I respond to that without hurting his feelings? He'd picked the wrong girl if he wanted emotional security.

I mean, sure, I cared about all my men. Hell, I'd lay down my life for them. They each completed me in some way and I couldn't imagine my future without them, but—

I sucked in a breath. I was an idiot. I wanted to spend all my time with them. I'd die for them. What the heck else did that mean except love?

I thought my upbringing meant I wasn't capable of it, that love wasn't something I knew how to give. But I'd been feeling it all this time and was just too scared to put a name on it.

I could still screw everything up. I hadn't had great role models when it came to relationships. And with all of us going into battle and facing death, it seemed like a bad time to strengthen our attachments. Talking about love wasn't going to help anything.

I pressed my body into his, wrapping my arms around his neck. "That's something every girl likes to hear." I brushed my lips over his. "Thank you, baby."

Did he wince? Well, I could get his mind off of my pathetic response. In the best, most satisfying way possible.

"Do you have any more secret meetings you have to disappear to?" I nibbled my way across his jaw.

His arms banded tighter around me. "No."

"Then I was thinking." I sucked at a patch of skin on his throat then scored it with my teeth.

Dante sucked in a sharp breath. He went hard behind his pants, his erection pressing against my belly.

My lips curved. "I was thinking that maybe I could help you with that whole vampire senses thing, like I helped with your super speed."

"And how are you going to do that?" His voice had dropped a register, and the sound of it curled around me like a caress.

I popped the top button of my jeans. Taking his hand, I pressed his palm to my stomach then eased it down.

He slipped beneath my panties. I moaned as he ran his finger along my slit, delving between my lips, finding me already wet.

"I could do this all night, but I don't see how it's going to help tap into my vampire senses."

With regret, I pulled his hand from my body and held it up between our faces. The scent of my need tinged the air. "Smell that."

Keeping his gaze pinned on mine, he bent his head and ran his tongue along his finger, tasting me.

My nipples pebbled. I forced myself to step back, away from him, and toward the door. "Give me a minute head start," I told him. "Then track me using only your sense of smell. No scrying spells tonight."

He prowled after me, step for step, as I backed toward the exit. "And what happens when I catch you?" He brought his hand to his nose, inhaling deeply, and the pointy edges of his incisors peeked out beneath his lip.

"You find me, you can have me." And with that, I spun and raced away.

I couldn't wait to be captured.

Chapter Twelve

I staggered into the gym, wishing the coffee I held in my hands could be mainlined into my veins. "You'd better have a damn good reason calling me here this early, Bane, or else I'm going to—"

He turned and stepped aside. Gareth stood next to him.

I shrieked like a little girl and flung myself at the demon, barely noticing as Bane used his magic to steady the mug I'd tossed in the air. I launched into Gareth's arms. His body had no give, but I didn't mind the pain. Gareth was here. Safe. That was worth the feeling of running into a brick wall.

He gripped my ass with one hand and buried his face in the crook of my neck. “You smell like him,” he growled.

“What?” I braced my hands on his shoulders and tried to sniff myself. I’d showered this morning.

He flicked his tongue out, zig zagging it up my neck, and I forgot about smelling bad.

“Can’t this wait until later?’ Bane asked, sounding bored.

“No,” Gareth and I said together.

Dante strolled into the gym, his own cup of coffee in his hand. “Oh. Great. The demon’s back.”

Gareth spun me around, pressing my back against his front and locking his arms around my waist. “She smells of you,” he grumbled before continuing that delightful business of his tongue on my neck.

“Smells of me, so probably tastes of me, too.” Dante stopped in front of us, his eyes twinkling. “Which means when you lick her, you’re tasting me, as well. I didn’t know I did it for you, big guy.” He ignored the demon’s growl and gave me a soft kiss. “Morning, baby.”

“Hi,” I said softly. I couldn’t lie. Having Gareth pressed against my back and Dante at my front felt really farkin’ good. I darted a glance at Bane.

The glimmer of longing disappeared as soon as he caught me looking. His arched eyebrow and condescending sneer took its place. "Now that we're all here, can we get down to business, or should I leave you three alone to waste more time?"

"Business." As much as I loved Gareth and Dante's hands on me, I didn't want to have another group nooky session if Bane wasn't there, too. It felt like betrayal.

"I have a potential name." Gareth slipped his hands under my shirt, rubbing his palms against my abdomen. It felt good until I realized what he was doing. Trying to cover Dante's scent with his own.

Okay, it still felt good, even though I didn't appreciate being the fire hydrant he was trying to pee on.

"There are rumors that Muythag Dak has been fortifying his holdings," Gareth said. "Food supplies, weaponry, all being shipped to his lands in unheard of numbers."

"Sounds like either a party we're missing out on," I joked, "or—"

"An army base." Bane crossed his arms over his chest, his face grim. "Dak would make sense. He's been quiet for a while, but he's a troublemaker at heart."

"Why does it make sense?" I asked. "Who's Moytag Dak?"

"*Muythag* Dak is a Utab demon, a cousin to my kind." Gareth gave my belly one more stroke then stepped back. "Legend says he was left by a witch twelve hundred years ago. He's had a grudge against the magical realm since then."

"This is all because someone got dumped?" My voice might have reached dog-whistle levels. I tried to lower its pitch. Ratcheting down my anger was another matter. "There's going to be a war with lots of deaths simply because this asshole couldn't get his dick wet?"

"It's not about sex." Dante took a sip of his coffee. "He was in love."

Bane was five steps too far away with my coffee so I snatched Dante's mug from him and downed his drink. More love talk. Last night Dante had wanted me to say it back to him. He'd provided me with several prime opportunities throughout the evening.

But I couldn't. The words wouldn't come. I had no idea how to walk that path. "I don't care. It's stupid. If I had my heart broken, I would drown it in a gallon of rocky road. I wouldn't plot for a millennium to subjugate a whole race of people." At least I hoped I wouldn't. I thought about what I'd do if any of my guys betrayed me, how my half-demon part would feel. I did have that inner bitch inside of me, waiting to come out.

Nope. I nodded. I'd be royally pissed, but I wouldn't go psycho-killer. That was a next-level crazy that even my demon side didn't approve of.

"If he's our man." A squiggle of black ink twined around Gareth's forearm. "I don't have confirmation on that. But I'll get it."

"How?" I asked.

"My father." Gareth widened his stance. "He knows everything that goes on in lower world. If large shipments were being sent to Dak's home, he'd be sure to get a cut of it."

"You were just there," I pointed out. "If he didn't tell you before, why do you think he would now?"

Gareth's gold eyes locked with mine. "I didn't press the issue before, not wanting a full confrontation. I will now."

My mouth went dry. "What all goes into a 'full confrontation?'" That didn't sound like something a person would want to get into with Lucifer, King of the Underworld.

"If I challenge him, it will be a battle to the death."

I was shaking my head before my lips could even more. "No. Absolutely not. It's not going to happen."

"Pet—"

"Don't 'pet' me." I planted my hands on my hips. "We are going into a war that could end the magical world. We need you in the ranks, not getting yourself killed before you'd even be useful."

"You're assuming I'd lose." His nostrils flared. "I won't."

"Which would only leave you with a bigger problem." Bane took a sip of my coffee. "Whoever kills Lucifer would then be responsible for managing lower world. A distraction we don't need."

I snort-laughed. Only Bane would call running hell a distraction. And I couldn't believe we were having this conversation. I shook my head. It all felt so surreal.

But it wasn't. This was now my life. And I wasn't going to let some stubborn, arrogant, sexy demon mess it up by getting himself killed. "You're not confronting your father, and that's final."

Gareth's lips twitched. "You think you have the power to stop me, pet?"

That sounded like a challenge I wanted to take. But also one I could lose. "Find another way."

Two black lines writhed up his neck. They bent, joining together into what I swore was a heart. I blinked, and it was gone, the lines wriggling back below his collar.

Gareth sighed. "My father is a bureaucrat at heart. There will be records. I need to go back and search his private rooms."

"What sort of records does the devil keep?" Dante asked.

Gareth shrugged. "He maintains records on every soul that comes to the lower world, and even on some of those he hopes will eventually come under his control. Anything he could profit by."

"If it's Dak, that could help us," Bane said.

"Yes." Gareth analyzed the white board we'd rolled into the gym, examining the Xs and Os we'd drawn for a mock battle.

"How?" I asked.

Dante came to me and dropped an arm around my shoulder.

Gareth glared. "Dak isn't well liked in the lower world. The past thousand years he's been a whiny bitch to his fellow demons. I should be able to recruit more of my kind to our cause."

"Our kind." I hooked my hand in Dante's back pocket, needing the contact.

Gareth frowned. "What?"

I looked at Dante, then Bane. "You didn't tell him?"

"I didn't think it was our place," Bane said.

Sure, now they found boundaries. I raised my chin. "Turns out my dad is a Glauxo demon. I'm one of your kind, too."

Gareth blinked. "That explains how you could understand Lucifer and me when we spoke in Chluxto." He checked his weapons. "Only those with demon blood can."

"Is that it? All you have to say?"

"What does it matter?" he said. "You're you, regardless of who or what your parents are."

And to him, it really was that simple. And...maybe it could be that simple for me, too. I hadn't changed. Only my perception of myself had.

"Well, before you return to lower world"—and didn't that thought just twist my stomach—"talk to me about the Root. Bane said you and Dante had some ideas about it."

"Nothing definite." Dante pulled me closer. "Accessing the In-Between is tricky. If your father is right, the Root of Corruption has been there for a long time. Perhaps it's best to let sleeping dogs lie."

I chewed my bottom lip. "But if it can take someone's power, maybe we can use it against Dak."

Bane scraped his palm across his jaw. "I'm gathering intel on those tests your father spoke of. Until we know what we're getting into, it's too dangerous."

I nodded. It was the same issue as Gareth fighting Lucifer. It was a risk to one of our lives when we were needed for the battle, with no assurances the pay-off would be of any use. "Agreed. Now," I began, looking at my men hopefully, "before Gareth leaves, any chance we can—"

The door to the gym banged against the wall. Ophelia and her friend, Rosamunde, hurried toward us. "Have you seen the news?" Ophelia asked, her face pale.

"No." My stomach dipped to my feet. "What's happened?"

She grabbed Rosamunde's hand. "It's London. We're under attack."

Chapter Thirteen

Today's training was more somber than it had ever been. I think a lot of the students felt the coming war had been nothing more than a game, but after the news this morning, it had become very real.

Eight hundred and fifty-six witches and warlocks were dead, and that number was expected to rise.

And the worst part was, they had been killed by other witches. The dark army had made their first formal strike, launching simultaneous attacks at Thornwood, an academy outside London, on the headquarters of a British-based white lodge, and on a magical hospital in Manchester.

Bane, Gareth, and Dante had spent the day refortifying Raven's defenses, before Gareth had left for lower world again. More and more students returned to the academy to join the fight, our group now too large to remain in the gym. We trained outside on the soccer fields. Lights had been conjured and floated above us in the darkening sky.

But no one wanted to leave. Everyone wanted to train until we dropped.

I spun the battle axe over my head and directed it through the air. It split the truck of a young oak. It took more effort to remove the axe and bring it careening back into my hand, but once I did, a student healed the split in the tree so I could use it as a target again.

Ophelia stalked up to me. "It's getting late. Have you thought about what to do for dinner and sleeping arrangements?"

The witch had been one of the hardest workers, surprising the hell out of me. She still gave me snotty comments, and I didn't know if when it came down to it that she wouldn't turn tail and run, but I had to give her props for her training ethic.

"What are you talking about?" I pressed the head of the axe into the earth and leaned on the handle. My right quad was cramping, and I hoped I could find one of my guys to give it a massage.

And do other things.

"There's still dry food in the kitchen and we all still have our rooms," I said.

"Dry food might have worked when it was just a motley group of students, but we have other people showing up." She waved her hand around the field, and for the first time I noticed the new faces. "Some professors have returned. Other witches who want to join the cause. This is your army." She sniffed. "You'd best provide for it."

The backs of my eyes burned. From gratitude for the extra support. From exhaustion. From fear, because this was all getting real for me, too. And I was the one who had to manage it.

I rubbed the back of my neck. "Yeah, I'll work something out. I don't suppose cook has returned?" I asked hopefully.

She snorted. "It's better he hasn't. You could stand to lose a few pounds." And with a flip of her caramel-brown hair, she sauntered away.

I hooked the axe's handle behind my head, holding onto it with both hands. I rested my head back against the wood shaft, closing my eyes.

There were empty staff rooms people could fill. But after that, we'd have to start doubling or tripling up. I'd free up my room and go stay with Dante. As for food, this was New Orleans. Surely we could hire a decent chef. I didn't know how we'd pay him, but I'd let Bane worry about that. For tonight, we'd—

"Sleeping on the job?" a familiar voice asked. "I knew she wouldn't be able to do this without us."

My eyes flew open. "Hazel? And Quincy!" I tossed the axe into the air and let it hover before dragging my friends into my arms. If Quincy's gurgling was any indication, I might have been choking them, but I was too excited to stop. "What are you doing here? Are you back for good? I've missed you."

Hazel patted my back. "Help you. Yes. Good." Her voice was a wheeze, and I finally released my python grip of their necks.

Three middle-aged people stood behind them. Two of them I recognized as Hazel's parents. The other woman must have been Quincy's mom. I stuck out my hand. "Hi, Ms. Quincy. I'm Delaney. I just love your son. I mean, not in that way, but in every other way that matters."

She chuckled as she squeezed my hand. "I've heard a lot about you. It's nice to know my son has such good friends." A shadow passed across her face. "I'm just sorry we had to meet under these circumstances."

"I can't believe we're facing these circumstances." Mrs. Willowtree leaned into her husband. "The prophecy had almost become a fairytale to my mind. That it's actually playing out now is, well, it's unbelievable."

"After what happened last night in England, we have to believe it." Hazel's widow's peak dipped low. "Nowhere is safe until we rid the world of this evil. That's why we're back. And our parents have come to join the army, too."

I was so happy to see them.

And so farkin' freaked out that they would be battling beside me. "You could hunker down somewhere, wait for the war to end." I had to offer it, take some of the responsibility for their lives off my shoulders. "I bet Hedwig would let you stay in her cottage."

"Hedwig?" Mr. Willowtree asked.

"Hedwig Bancroft, Druella Bancroft's sister," Hazel explained.

"You know the sister of the oracle who prophesied this mess." He took off his glasses and rubbed his eyes. "You have been busy." He didn't look happy about it, either. I was worried enough about my friends getting involved; I couldn't imagine how a parent would feel knowing their child was exposed to danger.

Well, how a normal parent would feel anyhow. My dad didn't give a shit, but the knowledge of his indifference didn't cut me quite so deeply anymore. For the first time, I had a family. None of them were blood, but Hazel and Quincy, Gareth and Dante and Bane, they were my family.

And I couldn't imagine any better.

I hooked my arm through Willow's and we joined the trail of people heading inside for dinner.

"Now, I have a very important question," I said to Hazel and Quincy's parents.

"Can any of you cook?"

Chapter Fourteen

"Told ya so." Hazel looked smug as she slurped down some noodles. Although her parents could cook, they'd emphatically stated they didn't want to. So we were in Hazel's room eating take out, the parentals watching the news, and Hazel, Quincy, and I sitting on the floor by her bed demolishing the leftovers.

"You said it was good." I pointed my chopsticks at her. "You didn't say it was freaking phenomenal. I mean, I couldn't put it down. I didn't go to sleep until four that morning because I had to finish it." Training that next day hadn't been fun, but the book Hazel had given me had been worth all the pain.

Hazel nudged Quincy. “I believe we have a new convert to the joys of reading.”

“I wouldn’t go that far,” I grumbled. I stabbed at a piece of pineapple in my carton. “I still probably would have preferred it in audio.” But if all Hazel’s recommendations were that good, then, yeah, reading was worth the slight headache it gave me.

“So what’s been going on since we left?” Hazel leaned forward, resting her elbows on her crossed legs. “The army is looking good. Small but good.”

I blew out a breath. The soccer field had been near full to bursting today, but it was only a couple hundred people out there. In terms of battle forces, we were small. But I didn’t think our opponent’s force could be much bigger. Only thirty-six former students had disappeared into their ranks, and I couldn’t imagine their recruitment had gone much easier than ours.

Of course, they were paying their mercenaries, and money always attracted people. We were just trying to survive.

“Bane is really hitting it out of the park with his tactics sessions.” He was becoming a bit too attached to his white board and didn’t appreciate me teasing him about it. So, of course, I teased him more. Someone had to take the piss out of him, an English saying he’d taught me and now regretted doing so. "We've created small squadrons and he's teaching all the squad leaders the military strategy he knows." Which was a surprising amount.

Well, maybe not too surprising. Bane had been preparing for this war for most of his life. I rubbed my breastbone. An entire life researching prophecies, searching for the Chosen One, prepping for battle. No wonder he was so serious.

"Tomorrow we're running drills, squad against squad, and we'll see how well our training has paid off," I said. "Gareth is still looking for confirmation that Muythag Dak is our bad guy. And Dante is working at controlling his vampire powers so he can be the ultimate badass."

"He's not the only one." Quincy broke open a fortune cookie and gave the white slip of paper to Hazel.

"Quincy's right," Hazel said. "If your moves with the battle axe are any indication, you've really upped your game." She scanned the fortune, crumpled it up and tossed it back at Quincy, smirking.

I raised my index finger, freezing the fortune in mid-air. I narrowed my eyes, feeling the heat well in my center before arcing to the paper. It burst into flame, the ashes swirling down to the carpet.

"Damn." Hazel nodded, impressed. "You really have come into your witch."

"It's bitch magic." I shrugged. "It used to come out when I was mad, but now I'm angry all the time."

Quincy frowned.

"Not a lot," I assured him. "Not enough to ruin my day. But I'm pissed that we all have to face this because some asshat wants to take over the world. So my inner bitch is always there, right under the surface. I've learned how to work with her."

I sounded confident, like I knew what I was doing. Like the woman they were all following wasn't full of shit. But I hadn't been put under real stress yet to test my new control. I was worried my magic would falter in the heat of battle.

Did I say worried? Hell, I was scared to death I'd freeze when put to the test and people would die. Myself included.

But I couldn't let that show. As Sun Tzu said, "You have to believe in yourself." I cleared my throat. "Hey, have either of you ever heard of the Root of Corruption?"

Hazel and Quincy glanced at each other and shook their heads.

"Oh." I spun my chopsticks over my open palm until one of them flew away into Hazel's hand.

"Are you going to tell us what it is or do we have to guess?" she asked.

I smiled sheepishly. "Sorry. It's a cup-like object. Maybe a bowl. Chalice? I'm going to go with chalice." I liked the way that word sounded. "Supposedly, if you drink someone's blood from the Root, you take their powers. My dad told me, Dante, and Bane about it. Suggested they use it to strip me of my powers so I couldn't be the Chosen One anymore." And couldn't destroy the world.

Hazel gasped. "So you wouldn't be able to save the world? No thanks."

My heart warmed. She sounded so certain that I would be on the side of right. Some of her confidence infused into me. I mean, I didn't want to destroy the magical world, so why would I? Even if I was part demon.

Quincy nudged Hazel with his elbow.

"You're right," she said. "Something like that could be useful. This Dak wants to strip the world of magic. What if we stripped him of his powers?"

"We don't know for sure Dak is behind this." I leaned against the bed and rubbed my happy stomach.

It had been too long since I'd eaten something full fat and delicious. "And this artifact is hard to get, apparently. Like deadly hard. The guys and I decided it's too dangerous to go for."

"Yet you're still asking about it," Hazel said.

I twisted my lips. "Yeah. I can't quite get it off my mind." Ever since my dad had mentioned it, the idea of using it had gnawed on me like a dog on an old bone. Maybe it was because of its similarity to the Holy Grail, a cup that bestowed great power. It fired all my Indiana Jones questing instincts. It beckoned to me like a chocolate-cherry cheesecake.

Perhaps I just wanted to focus on something, anything, else.

"Can you look into it?" I asked Hazel and Quincy. They were masters at research. "I'd feel better if we knew more about it."

"On it." Hazel yawned. "Well, first thing tomorrow we're on it."

I stretched and rolled to my feet. Tomorrow could either go really well, or make me realize that we had no chance in hell of winning, depending on how the mock battles went. But tonight, I had Dante to curl up with.

But first, there was something I had to know. "Have you heard if they're making a movie out of our book?"

CHAPTER FIFTEEN

Bane, Dante, and Killough stood below me, each man had his arms crossed over his chest and a serious look hardening his face.

Their fighting expressions. I knew it well. Had perfected it during my time in the cage. I swung my feet. My legs dangled from the magnolia tree limb I was perched on. The aerial position gave me a better view of the battlefield, aka the grounds of Raven.

A ball of flame lit the sky over the pool, and I peered in that direction. "Damn it," I muttered. "I need binoculars."

"Or you can do a spell for remote viewing," a voice said in my ear.

I shrieked and spun on my branch. "Gareth!" I didn't know if I was pissed at him for scaring me or ecstatic to see him. "I— oh shit!" I wind-milled my arms, off-balance.

Gareth reached for me, but I was already falling. A branch scraped my cheek; my sneaker was dragged from my foot. I gathered my intention, tried to conjure my levitation spell, but strong arms had already wrapped around me, stopping me from going splat on the ground.

Bane looked down at me, looked up at Gareth, and frowned. "Now isn't the time to fool around."

"We weren't fooling around." I twined my arms around Bane's neck. The faint aroma of licorice and cherrywood curled around me, and I snuggled closer. "Gareth scared the bejeezus out of me, popping up on the next branch."

The demon in question swung down from the tree, landing before us as nimbly as a cat. "Sorry, pet. I thought you had better balance."

"I have excellent balance. On the ground." I scanned Gareth's body. Everything seemed in place. No visible wounds. My demon was okay.

Bane dropped my feet to the ground and stepped back.

Since my hands were laced around his neck, I moved with him.

He arched one perfectly-groomed eyebrow.

My face flushed. I released my grip and took my hands from his body.

I might have smoothed my palms over his firm chest along the way. Sue me.

"No one saw that, right?" I glanced around, but none of the fighters were in the immediate vicinity. "Me falling out of the tree?"

"We all saw it," Killough said.

"I mean no one who's going to be taking orders from me."

Bane pulled a handkerchief from his pocket. He tilted my chin up and dabbed at my cheek, frowning. The handkerchief came away with spots of red.

I touched the sting to my cheek. "Awesome." I sighed and turned to Gareth. "You're back. And if you'd appeared normally instead of scaring me, I would have given you a welcome hug."

He dragged me into his arms. "I'm taking the hug anyway."

I smiled into his black T-shirt, listening to his heart's rapid beat. Something inside me settled, as it always did when I was with all three of my men. It was like a gear, clicking into place.

"Are you going to tell us what you found out," Dante said, "or are you just going to manhandle Delaney?"

I gave him one last squeeze and stepped back. "Okay. Debrief us."

Gareth's lips twitched.

"Yes," I said. "I'm getting down with the military lingo. Now talk."

"It's confirmed. Dak is behind this." Gareth ran his hand over his shaved head. "And Lucifer knew all along."

"How certain is this confirmation?" I shoved my hands into my back pockets. "Eighty percent? Ninety-five? Ninety-nine percent sure?"

"It's confirmed." Gareth didn't elaborate, but then, he'd never been the chatty type.

"What evidence do you have?" Dante asked.

"A signed and notarized contract between Lucifer and Dak." Four black lines circled angrily on Gareth's forearm. "My father not only is getting kickbacks for sending witches to him as mercenaries, but he's also agreed to loan out souls under his control to fight for Dak."

"And Lucifer has this written down in a contract?" That seemed a bit stupid. I couldn't imagine the mafia had written agreements detailing all the laws they were breaking.

Gareth shrugged. "Lucifer likes paperwork. And the vaults he keeps his important contracts in are near impossible to access."

But Gareth had. My chest expanded. My guys really did rock.

Bane seemed determined to be the downer of the group. "How many souls are against us?"

"Many."

"But, these are dead people, right?" I rubbed my forehead. "Spirits. Ghosts. How can they even fight?"

"When souls return from lower world, they are what humans call poltergeists," Bane said. "An invisible foe that can control matter on this plane to varying degree." He pinched the bridge of his nose and closed his eyes. "This doesn't help our odds."

I placed my hand on his lower back. I know he didn't like crossing his stupid boundaries, but he looked like he needed any small comfort. Damn it, I needed the connection. As if our battle wouldn't be hard enough, we now had evil Caspers to deal with.

"Our kind doesn't do well with spirits." If possible, Killough's skin looked even paler. "This might dissuade some vampires from fighting on our side."

"Why?" I leaned closer into Bane, encouraged that he hadn't stepped away or given me that disapproving look he'd perfected.

"Because vampires don't have souls." Dante swallowed, his Adam's apple bobbing. "When vamps die, there is no afterlife for them."

"And because we have no souls, when a spirit encounters us, it can take over our bodies." Killough squeezed Dante's shoulder. "You're only half vamp. This shouldn't affect you."

I didn't like the sound of that 'shouldn't.' I wanted a 'wouldn't.' This was Dante he was speaking of. I wanted certainty.

And what did having a soul even mean if someone who didn't have one could still love and have a sense of right and wrong and duty. I looked at Killough, then Dante. And if they died in this battle, did that mean that was it for them? Lights out, no afterlife?

Dante stepped to my other side, threading his fingers through mine.

I leaned my head on his shoulder, still keeping my contact with Bane. It would destroy me if anything happened to these men.

"There is some good news," Gareth said.

"Finally," I muttered.

"I've recruited many demons to our side." Gareth placed his finger under my chin and raised my face to his. "They'll be here tomorrow. Our numbers have grown significantly."

I don't know whether it was his words or the fact that some part of me was touched by all three of my men, but my fear evaporated. Yes, I was still worried, and the responsibility of so many lives weighed on me.

But I could finally take a full breath again. We had a just cause. Talented and deadly people on our side. I didn't see how we could lose.

Gareth stroked my cheek with his thumb. "Even better, Dak has made a mistake. He is in talks with the black lodge of Ottawa to hire more witches. He's agreed to leave lower world in three days to speak with them on their own turf. It's an opportunity we shouldn't miss."

"Black lodge?" I snort-laughed. Yes, there were white lodges of good witches so the opposite shouldn't come as a surprise. But it sounded so mustache-twirling silly. And in Canada? The land of Tim Horton's donuts, hockey, and the friendliest people on the planet? Nothing evil should come from there.

"Do you have a plan?" Bane asked Gareth.

"The start of one." Gareth trailed his fingertips down my neck, lighting up my nerve endings. "It needs work."

Killough cleared his throat. He glanced at me and Dante leaning against each other, my hand still rubbing Bane's back. Gareth doing whatever he was doing to my throat. "I'll leave you to it. I need to tell my people of these latest developments. Let me know when you've decided on a strategy." He took a normal-speed step, two, before going into vamp mode and zipping away.

Like he couldn't wait to get away from the four of us and whatever touchy-feely thing was going on.

We'd managed to embarrass a vampire.

My lips tilted up. Which was fine since it left us alone. "So, in three days this will be over," I said softly.

"Perhaps." Bane locked eyes with me. The longing I saw there stole my breath. He raised his hand as if to brush my hair from my forehead but stopped before he made contact. His face closed down and he stepped away.

My own hand dropped.

"But it will take more than one battle to win a war." He looked away, and the layers of meaning to his words must have struck him as they struck me.

"Not if we fight this battle well." Gareth stepped to my other side, taking the place Bane had vacated. He didn't seem to want to stop touching me, and as he'd been risking his life in underworld for too long, my body agreed with his sentiments.

But it still wanted the one man's touch it was missing. And I was starting to get pissy that I didn't have it.

Yes, I was a greedy wench for wanting all three men. But I knew all three men wanted me, too. And I knew we could find a way to make it work. Bane's professional reasons for keeping his distance no longer applied. I wasn't his student. He was just being stubborn.

He ran a hand through his dark hair, looking as frustrated as I felt. My irritation morphed into sympathy. Sometimes it was hard allowing yourself to have something good. I knew all about not feeling worthy of love. About not allowing yourself to have something great because you were scared to lose it. So I'd let his bull-headedness slide.

For now. But my patience with his nonsense was wearing thin. We could all be happy together; I knew it.

And with a war in front of us, happiness seemed like a rare and precious gift, not one to be wasted.

The war. I blew out a breath. Maybe I should focus on getting through that first, and then plot my sexy seduction of Bane. "This plan of yours." I left the comfort of Gareth's and Dante's heat and plopped to the earth, sitting cross-legged. "Let's hear it."

We sat together and plotted until the sun went down. And then we went to the gym and Bane's whiteboard and plotted some more. It was early in the morning before we had a strategy we were all happy with.

I rolled onto my toes and stretched my hands into the air, my back cracking with a satisfying pop. "So we're agreed? We start training for this tomorrow? Err, today?"

Bane hid his yawn behind his hand. "Agreed. I'll bring in the squad leaders after I get a couple hours sleep."

I nodded, biting my tongue so I didn't say something stupid, something like asking to join him for his nap. "Right."

I examined the board. It would work. It had to work. In three days' time, all this would be over. "One last thing," I said as we wandered to the door. I pointed to the scabbed over scratch on my cheek. "Can we tell everyone I got this fighting? 'Cause attacked by tree branch really doesn't inspire confidence in the troops."

Chapter Sixteen

"Ms. Jones!" Bane's voice caused my shoulders to hunch toward my ears.

Of course he'd find me now. Every moment of the past two days had been filled with drills, negotiations with demons, more drills, interspersed only with brief periods of napping and eating. I'd played the role of the Chosen One for every moment of the past fifty hours.

Until now. When I'd decided to let my guard down for five damn minutes with Hazel and Quincy. Now was when he found me for a convo.

I splashed Hazel in the face with one more burst of rainbow-swirled water. We were underwear-dipping in the east pond on Raven grounds. The multi-colored water was thanks to Quincy. Hazel was responsible for the statue of the naked centaur spinning above us and spritzing out water from his enormous, er, centaur bits.

Bane stood on the shore, hands gripping his lean hips, a muscle ticking in his jaw. "May I speak with you? Now."

"I'd better handle this," I said to my friends. "I'll catch up with you in a bit."

Hazel wrung out the tips of her hair. "See you later." She stalked out of the pond, not bothering to cover up any of her skin.

Bane kept his gaze fixed on my face.

Quincy wasn't so strong. He darted looks at the wet cotton that covered her butt and breasts, his cheeks flushing red. But his gaze kept getting dragged back.

"Sayonara," Hazel called, picking up her clothes and wandering off, Quincy on her six.

I sank into the water until it covered my chin. "Well?"

A raven spiraled overhead, and Bane followed its path. "Will you come out of there? I don't want to talk to you while you're..." He flapped his hand up and down.

I stood to full height, baring my sports bra and midriff. The soaked cotton clung to my breasts. A cool breeze peaked my nipples.

That raven must have been putting on quite the aeronautic display, because Bane refused to peel his gaze from it.

I stepped one foot forward. Another. Until the water skimmed my thighs. "Something bothering you, Professor." I threw the title out like an insult. It stood between us like a wall, one I was fully prepared to bulldoze.

"Nothing's bothering me," he said, voice gruff.

I moved until the water swirled around my ankles. "No? Because you came here to tell me something yet now you're being awfully quiet. Am I too distracting, wet and half-naked?"

He dropped his eyes, looking determined to keep his gaze on my face.

I was determined to break his control.

"We need to speak about your frivolity." He swallowed. "We attack tomorrow. You can't waste time splashing about."

"I need to be in fighting form," I argued. I reached my arms up, arching my back. "The swim relaxed my muscles."

Bane refused to look down at my awesome rack. He was made of steel, damn it.

I dropped my arms, feeling silly. I wasn't the seductress type apparently. If only I could arm bar him into submission. I tilted my head. Maybe—

A loud splash erupted behind me. I launched forward, throwing myself at Bane and taking him down. I covered his body from attack, my back tensing.

His hands warmed my waist. "What are you doing?"

I peered over my shoulder. Waves rippled over the pond but no threat lurked. "Uh, protecting you?"

"From a statue dropping into a pond?"

"Oh." Hazel must have gone out of distance for her magic. My cheeks heated. But I didn't move.

Bane's body underneath mine felt too damn good.

I pressed my hand to his chest. "We fight tomorrow." In just a couple of hours in fact. They wanted to get into place before Dak arrived at the lodge so it was to be an early morning assault.

"Yes." Bane trailed his fingers up my spine. I don't even think he realized he was doing it, but he craved my touch as much as I did his.

"We might not all survive."

His body tensed. "You'll survive. I'll make sure of it."

I traced the line of his jaw. "That's sweet, but not my point."

"What is your point?"

I wiggled a little higher on his body so my mouth was level over his. "We can't rely on a future. Don't you think we should live for today?" If I died tomorrow, I would die a whole lot happier having known the touch of each of my men.

If possible, his body went even harder. Or at least, parts south did. The ridge of his erection pressed against my belly, and my mouth went dry.

Bane placed his hands on my shoulders and tried to nudge me away.

I settled more firmly into his body.

"You're getting me wet," he said.

"It's only fair." I lowered my head and nipped his jaw. "You make me wet every time you open your mouth." I trailed my lips up to his ear, using the tip of my tongue to mark him. "I love your accent, the bossy things you say. The way you can sound condescending, worried, and frustrated as hell, all at the same time."

He groaned. "I only sound that way with you." His hands roamed low, gripping my ass and pulling me tight as he rocked against me.

"School's out, Bane." I dug my fingers into his thick hair. "There's no reason why we can't have this. Stop denying yourself. Stop denying me."

I was on my back before my next breath. Bane pressed my hands into the earth beside my head. "This is wrong."

I hooked my foot around his calf, opening myself further to him. "Then let's be wrong together." My breath came out in shudders. I'd never wanted anything as I wanted Bane in this moment. If he denied me now, denied us, I didn't know what I'd do. He would—

He lowered his head and covered my mouth with his own.

Everything went silent around us. I no longer heard the water lapping on the shore, the birds calling to each other in the sky, or the wind soughing through the leaves. It was as though we were in a bubble, Bane and I, and his lips on mine were the only things that mattered.

Bane was kissing me. And it was heaven.

He took his time exploring the outer edges of my lips, tonguing the slight seam in the middle of my bottom lip, before slowly, leisurely, easing his way inside my mouth. It was like he thought we had an eternity to do nothing but kiss, and he was going to eke out every second of it.

I moaned at the first brush of his tongue along mine. Tingles started at the back of my neck, and rippled through my body, hardening my nipples and curling my toes.

Bane was kissing me. Touching me. And through the pleasure, my emotions welled. A tear rolled down my face.

I wrapped my arms around his back and deepened the kiss. I ignored the clutch to my heart and focused on the way his tongue curled around mine, how each thrust of that marvelous organ foreshadowed what was to come.

Sinjin farkin' Bane was kissing me, and I wasn't going to let anything ruin that, especially not my squishy feelings.

He skimmed his palm up my ribs, his large hand cupping my breast. He thumbed my nipple over my bra, and we both groaned.

"Sinjin." I fumbled with the button of his slacks. "I've wanted you for so long."

He gripped my wrist, stilling my hand. His mouth hovered over mine, his breath gusting across my abraded lips. "Wait."

Wait? Wait?! We'd been waiting for months. I tugged on my hand, but his grip tightened.

"No." He closed his eyes. "This is wrong. I can't do it."

I let out a sound between a whimper and a scream. "There is nothing wrong about this. Nothing wrong about how we feel." He was mine, just as Dante and Gareth were. We were right together. I knew it in my bones.

He pushed himself off of me, and I shivered from the loss of his heat. He straightened his damp jacket. "I'm sorry. I shouldn't have acted such."

"Why?" I cried. "Why deny something we both want? We both need?"

He raked his fingers through his hair. "I can't make love to a woman, not if I...." He shook his head. "I have to remain detached. I'm sorry, Delaney."

And he left me. Hot. Horny. And frustrated as hell.

And so, so sad. I curled into a ball. Bane thought he might have to kill me. Didn't he know his heart would break whether or not we slept together first? He would hate himself forever. Another reason I couldn't allow myself to become a force for evil.

I thumped the back of my head into the dirt. My body was revved, in fight or fuck mode, and the latter was no longer on the menu.

I rolled to my feet and yanked on my clothes. We left for Canada in nine hours. Theoretically, I still had time to find Dante or Gareth and work off some of my lust, but it wouldn't be fair to them. I couldn't just transfer my desire, my hurt, from one man to another.

Okay, Gareth might be happy to act as substitute. He'd probably take it as a challenge to rid my mind of Bane. But it felt wrong to me.

I trudged my way back to the school. I had nine hours to finalize any last details, sharpen my weapons, prepare myself. Adrenalin and hormones coursed my body, making me hyper-focused and putting me on edge.

I was in the perfect mindset for battle.

Go-time couldn't come soon enough.

Chapter Seventeen

A stone dug into my shin. I swear I'd moved every bit of rock from my hiding spot, but when I knelt, another sharp bastard poked into me.

Waiting for Dak to arrive was not only super boring, but uncomfortable as hell.

"How much longer?" Hazel whispered. She, Quincy, and I, along with two other witches, held position on the north corner of the castle outside Ottawa which the black lodge used as their headquarters. Dante, Gareth, and Bane each had possession of their own corner of the three-story stone fortress.

I gritted my teeth. Hazel was like one of those annoying kids in the back of a car asking if we were there yet every five minutes. “I don’t know. It’s not like Dak is texting me when he leaves.”

Hazel huffed and burrowed deeper into Quincy’s side.

I blew out a long breath. I glanced from Hazel, to the side entrance we would enter when Dak arrived, back to Hazel. “Fine,” I muttered. “I’ll go find one of my guys and see if we have any updated information.”

Arms wrapped around me from behind. “You called?”

I just stopped my elbow from slamming into Dante’s ribs. “Don’t be sneaking up on me,” I whisper-hissed. Snuggling back into his chest probably took the bite out of my words, but I craved his heat. Ottawa at four in the morning was damn nippy. And why the hell did bad guys do their business so farkin’ early? I didn’t expect to be so tired and grumpy for my first war.

“What are you doing here?” I asked Dante. “I thought you were going to text when we were to move in.”

He hesitated. “We agreed we didn’t want you going in alone.”

“We?” I asked the same time Hazel said, “Alone?”

She scowled, and pointed at the rest of the squad. “We’re not Wiccans here. We’ve got Delaney’s back.”

"Gareth, Bane, and I," he said to me. He merely shrugged apology to Hazel.

Okay, I definitely had mixed feelings about that one. I was supposed to be the leader, and having a boyfriend guarding my back wasn't very commanding. On the other hand, having a boyfriend watching my back was pretty sweet. Frankly, I wanted as much back-up as possible.

"Who's leading your squad?" I asked.

"Grimaldo." Dante rested his chin on my shoulder. "He knows the plan. They can go in without me."

I rubbed my thumb along his hand at my waist. "Bane couldn't have been happy you left your position, that we deviated from the plan."

"It was his idea."

"Oh." Was it because he cared so much about me, or because he thought I'd fuck it all up?

Or that I'd go rogue and destroy our side?

"What's wrong?" Dante's question was murmured so low no one else could hear.

I turned so I was just about sitting in his lap. "Nothing. It's just..." I bit my lip. "Do you think...?" I blew out a breath. "Never mind." Dante accepted my relationships with the other guys, but it wasn't fair to include him in my drama with Bane. He might know how I felt about the other two, but I didn't want to rub it in his face, either.

He stood, pulling me up along with him. He drew me away a couple of feet, into a recess in the stone wall. "What's wrong?"

I gave him a tight smile, useless in the dark. "It's not about this battle. It's not important. We need to focus."

"And when we get the call, we will. Until then, talk." He brushed a strand of hair off my cheek.

I swallowed. "It's Bane. Sinjin. He and I, uh, had a moment. We kissed." And dry-humped like teenagers. I'd felt every delicious inch of how much he'd wanted me. "And then he ran like I'd told him I had the clap."

I dropped my forehead to his shoulder. "I know you don't want to hear this. I'm sorry I can't make up my mind between you guys, but I want you all. I lo-like all three of you. But Bane won't let me in. I don't think he ever will, and it's breaking my heart."

Dante gripped the back of my neck, the pressure reassuring. He kissed my temple, showing no judgment, no anger, only acceptance.

Why couldn't I settle on having just him? Dante was damn near perfect. We were amazing together. If I'd never met Gareth or Bane, Dante and I would be the happiest of couples. Why wasn't he enough?

"I'm so sorry," I said, my eyes burning.

"Don't be." He raised my face and pressed his forehead to mine. "I have to be honest. I wasn't happy about it at first. But..." He loosed a long breath. "But I've come to accept it. Appreciate it even. We all fit different needs. We can all give you something unique. And you deserve everything. I think the four of us were meant to be a unit, as odd and annoying as some parts of that unit might be."

My lips curved up.

His voice went serious again. "Besides, if something happens to me, I want there to be someone else who will take care of you the way you deserve. Gareth would do anything for you, and for that, I'll always be grateful. And Bane..."

"Yes?" My heart tripped. Dante wasn't a seer, but his opinion on my future, our future, with Bane meant a lot.

"If it's meant to be, he'll come around. I see the expressions on both of your faces when you look at each other. I think it's meant to be." He pulled back so there was some space between us, but his hands still surrounded my face, his thumbs rubbing my cheeks. "But now you need to focus. You can't be worried about any of us when we attack Dak."

"You don't think there's a chance he'll surrender when he finds himself surrounded?" I'd asked this question before, never getting the answer I liked.

I still didn't. Dante snorted-laughed. "Good one. You definitely need watching, woman, and the job is bigger than just one man." He turned me around and nudged me back to our squad. "Now, if you want—"

Dante's and my cell phones buzzed. We looked at each other and nodded. I took a deep breath and knelt by my team. "We just got the signal," I told them. "It's go-time."

Chapter Eighteen

The portal was larger than any I'd ever seen. Wide enough for the five demons and two witches to come through, side by side. And tall enough to let Dak step under without bending his head, and that was saying something.

Muythag Dak was huge. At least eight feet tall and built like a fire truck. Had I thought Gareth looked intimidating when I'd first met him? Next to Dak, he looked like a teddy bear. Nope, not even that. Like a baby sloth, something completely harmless and adorable.

Dak had dark green skin, with scales that shimmered. Two long teeth jutted from his upper jaw like tusks. His eyes were round and unblinking, reminding me of the tweakers who used to hang around my fights. And his nose...

I swallowed. Well, he didn't really have one. Just two slashes above his mouth that trickles of black sludge oozed from.

It was one hundred to twelve, I reminded myself. They just had the five demons, the two witches they'd brought, and the five witches of the lodge. Due to the size of the castle, we'd limited our forces to thirty inside the fortress and seventy out, but now I was thinking that might not be enough.

We should have brought everyone we had.

"This interruption is"—a warlock wearing a long black cloak eyed me like I was shit on his shoe—"unwelcome."

We'd streamed into the room after the portal had activated, not as stealthily as I'd have liked, but we now surrounded the lodge members and Dak and his crew. Our force did look fierce, I had to admit. Our hands were raised and glowing, ready to strike, our resting witch faces looking somewhere between 'I want to rip your head off and eat it' and 'mmm, blood tastes good.'

I only wished Dak would look a little surprised at our entrance. A bit of fear wouldn't go amiss, either.

Bane stepped forward. "This interruption, as you call it, is necessary. Muythag Dak, son of Amio, we come to arrest you for your plot against the magical world. Come with us quietly, and there will be no bloodshed."

Dak grinned, his teeth glimmering in the light from the torches that lined the room. "But I like bloodshed. Especially of tasty little things that squeal." He pointed a clawed finger at Ophelia, who managed to look both bad-ass and high class in her black, skinny jeans and burgundy cowl-neck sweater. "I'll start with that one."

Ophelia paled but held firm. She definitely had her own kind of bitch power, and while I found it irritating when directed at me, I could appreciate it now.

I stepped forward, a short sword in one hand. Gareth had argued the space we would be fighting in would be too confined for the battle axe, and sadly, he'd been right. "The only blood that will flow will be yours and your friends." I figured Dak was a lost cause at trying to reason with, so I looked at the witches of the black lodge. "He wants to destroy witches and warlocks. Destroy magic. That includes you. Why are you helping him?"

The five black-hooded heads leaned towards each other, silently communicating. "We've made no agreements yet," one of them said. "We were waiting to hear his terms before you interrupted."

They looked to Dak.

He shrugged, a scale drifting off his arm and landing on the floor. "I only want to destroy some magic. The annoying, good kind. I'm sure you can appreciate that."

They nodded.

"Fools." Gareth stepped to my side. "You might not be the first ones he comes for, but come for you he will."

"He wants all magic destroyed," Dante said. He flanked my other side. "If a war comes, no one will be spared."

Another cloaked figure leaned forward. "Then why do so many of our kind fight for his side?"

"Immediate wealth outweighs future troubles for the weak-minded," Bane said. "There are many fools who think Dak's petty quest for vengeance will end before he gets to them. Don't be as foolish as the mercenaries he's hired."

Dak pressed a hand to his chest, the skin around his knuckles cracking. "Petty? Moi? You wound me."

I tightened my grip on my sword. Oh, I was going to wound him. I couldn't wait to wound him. "It's pathetic you're doing all this over a woman. FYI, maybe if you'd used some lotion, your girlfriend wouldn't have left you. Your scaly skin is nasty."

He turned on me, growing larger before my eyes. His head scraped the ceiling. His gaze was as hot as lava. "You dare?" he thundered.

I took a step toward him. "Hell yes, I dare. I might be new to the witch world, but I'll be damned if I let some whiny, emo demon destroy it." I rubbed a knuckle under my eye and feigned crying. "Did the mean witch hurt your feewings?" I said in a childlike voice. "Did she give your heart a boo boo?"

Bane angled his body between mine and the demon. Gareth stepped forward and Dante behind, forming a triangle around me. Like they knew I'd gone too far and had become target numero uno.

Good. I wanted his wrath to be directed at me. I wasn't going to let him touch any of my friends, not if I could help it.

Hazel snorted behind me. "He's like a sad Taylor Swift, making everything about his ex."

Dak swung his head her way.

That was one of the problems with having snarky friends. They were funny as hell, but tended to get themselves in trouble. I should know.

"Hey!" I brought his attention back to me. "Are we going to do this? We have seventy more people outside, just waiting to come in and get their piece of the action. You can fight back and let each of us have our jollies. We'll take turns and knock you about like demon whack-a-mole. Or you can tell your friends goodbye and come with us quietly."

Dante's white lodge had built a prison cell, just for him. I couldn't wait to stuff him inside and get on with the rest of my life.

Dak grinned, and a shiver skittered down my spine. Even surrounded by my men and my friends, a ripple of unease wormed its way inside of me.

"Seventy witches outside." Dak crossed his arms over his sequoia-sized chest.

"Yes, and the thirty in here." I waved my hand at the witches and warlocks ringing the room. "We clearly have you outnumbered. Don't be stupid."

"He was right," Dak said. "You really did think your pathetic army would be sufficient."

We all went silent, mulling over his words.

Finally, Bane asked, "Who is he?"

The portal shimmered. One cloven hoof stepped into the room, followed by another.

I looked up past furry legs, past an alabaster stomach and torso, into familiar gold eyes.

Gareth's eyes.

"I said so." Lucifer spread his arms wide and closed his eyes. Shimmering lights flickered outside the windows as portal after portal popped open. "And my numbers are much more than a hundred."

My stomach dropped to the floor. Even as more and more portals opened outside, Lucifer's demons and witches flooded in through the portal in our room.

We thought we had laid the perfect trap. It turned out the trap had closed around us.

Chapter Nineteen

"Lucifer." Gareth clenched his hands. "The finder's fees weren't enough for you. You had to get on Dak's payroll, too."

The ruler of lower world chuckled. "You always did think small. I'm not working for Dak. He's working for me."

Gareth took a step forward. "But I found—"

"What I wanted you to find." Lucifer examined his nails. "Creating a fake paper trail isn't difficult."

"Why?" Bane narrowed his eyes. "After millennia of peace between the worlds, why launch an attack now?"

Lucifer shrugged. "Power. Riches. Mayhem. Do I need another reason?"

There was more to it than that. There had to be. "You rule an entire realm. You're powerful. Uber-wealthy. Gareth said you were nothing more than a bureaucrat. Why change from grift to fighting?"

He smiled. And if I thought Dak's smile was scary, Lucifer's was downright terrifying. "Don't you know, little one? Bureaucrats are the most vicious beasts of all."

An eyebrow twitch was the only warning I got before a force slammed into my chest. I flew back, knocking into fellow witches and taking them down with me.

It was on. Gareth roared. Dante shouted my name. The room filled with sounds of battle.

"Get up." Hazel pulled on my arm. She shot a worried glance at Quincy, who stood sentry above us.

I blinked, willing my eyes to focus. Whatever magic Lucifer had thrown at me had left my brain cloudy and my gaze blurring.

Or maybe that had come from knocking my head into the floor.

I pushed up onto one hand. "Go. Fight. I'll be okay."

A witch I knew, someone I'd smiled at in the halls of Raven but whose name I couldn't remember, screamed and collapsed on the floor ten feet from us.

"Go!" I didn't need their handholding, not when it left them distracted and vulnerable.

I pushed up to my feet, locking my knees, and nodded at Hazel.

She nodded back before spinning and taking a position at Quincy's back. Her face was hard as she found a demon, targeted him, and launched a binding spell.

I found my sword on the ground, relieved I hadn't skewered anyone, and swiped it up.

Hazel and Quincy would be okay. They had to be.

I looked for Lucifer. He was the leader of this army. He was my target.

If I could farkin' get to him.

The room was so crowded now it was hard to even raise a hand to spell. Much too crowded to do anything more with my sword than make short, poking motions, which I did with great enthusiasm. A red-skinned demon yelped when I stabbed the back of his leg. He turned around swinging. I ducked and zapped him with an immobilization spell. His body as hard as a statue, he slowly toppled over, taking down another demon in his wake.

I used the path he cleared and got five feet closer to my target. Just thirty left to go.

"Jesus, I'll never get to him," I muttered, dropping to a knee and slashing the Achilles tendon on something blue and furry.

Dante knelt next to me, chest heaving. "You okay?" He flicked his wrist, and a mercenary witch bounced off the ceiling.

I swiped the back of my hand across my cheek, and it came away red with blood. "Just peachy. We need to focus our attack on Lucifer. If we can get to him."

Dante grabbed my wrist and stood. "Come on." He wrapped an arm around my waist. "I'll get us there. Just hold on to—" His body went rock hard against mine, and my heart stuttered thinking he'd been spelled.

But then I followed the direction of his gaze. My mouth dropped open. "What is that?" Another shadowy figure oozed from the ceiling and dropped into the room, joining the first. It was amorphous, and disappeared when I looked directly at it.

"Spirits." His voice was a harsh rasp.

Hazel cried out. I craned my head, but didn't see her. I did see the four-foot snake-like demon sneaking up on us, and threw an itching spell at him. He blinked, rubbed his skin, then fell to the ground, writhing.

I put my hand on Dante's chest. "You're half-witch. They can't hurt you." I hoped.

"We're about to find out," he said, grim, and set me aside.

One of the dark forms rushed at him.

"No!" I leapt in front of Dante and felt an icy caress as the spirit went through me. I spun, and my shoulders sagged in relief when the soul passed through Dante, as well.

It tried again, but couldn't stay in Dante's body. It shrieked, then spun up to the ceiling. It knocked over a candle from a chandelier, the flame burning out before it hit the ground.

Yeah, the little poltergeist could have fun with that. We had much bigger fish to fry.

Dante grinned and shook his head. "I really thought—" His face went slack, his gaze tracking the other spirit. "Shit. Killough!" he yelled in warning.

But it was too late. The vampire turned just as the soul enveloped his body, settling in.

Killough's face contorted. His limbs twitched. An anguished groan was torn from his mouth.

One second Dante was beside me, the next he was standing in front of his mentor. I fought my way towards them, hacking a limb here, spelling a demon there. I saw Bane circle Dak from the corner of my eye, but kept fighting my way toward Dante and Killough.

Battle, it turned out, was a lot like triage. I had to prioritize who to help.

And who to leave to fend for themselves.

"Delaney!" Quincy's voice screamed a warning, and I ducked instinctively.

A heavy mace swung over my head, missing me by inches. I growled. While I could appreciate the old school choice of weapon, the hairy bastard who'd swung it at me would have to be put down. My pulse raced. I was getting tired of this bullshit.

Quincy landed a binding spell. I sliced off the thing's fingers, its weapon falling to the floor. I nodded to my friend. We worked rather well together. I opened my mouth to ask about Hazel, when Killough appeared before us. He bent and picked up the mace.

"Thanks," he said, then swung the weapon full-force at Quincy's head.

My hand shot out, energy flowing through me, and Quincy's feet were pulled out from under him. He fell to the floor, Killough's swing passing harmlessly over him.

Dante was on Killough in an instant, wrestling for the weapon. They flew into the ceiling, raining chips of stone down.

I stuck out my hand. Quincy took it, but gave me a reproachful look as I pulled him up.

"I know," I said. "I should have pulled Killough's feet out from under him. I didn't think. It just happened."

A large section of plaster fell from the ceiling, hitting us in the shoulder and back, and we both went down again.

I kicked free of the debris and rolled to my knees. And froze.

Killough stood above Quincy, mace pressed into his chest, two of the iron spikes digging into my friend's skin, drawing blood.

The vampire shook. "I can't...fight it...much longer."

Dante landed in front of me. "Yes you can. You have to."

The vampire smiled, his fangs long. "You know. Once a spirit takes hold..." He twisted his neck, groaning as he dug the mace deeper into Quincy.

I scrambled forward, but Dante held me back. "He could crush him in an instant."

I locked gazes with Quincy. For as little as he spoke, his eyes said everything he felt. Fear. Pain. Acceptance. Disappointment. He searched the room, and I knew he looked for Hazel. Wanting hers to be the last face he saw.

"You're not dying," I yelled at him. There was no way I could watch my friend get killed right in front of me.

Dante slid his hand down my wrist. He took the sword from my loose grip.

Pain slashed across my back, and I threw a spell over my shoulder, not really caring if it landed or not.

"Drop the mace." Dante took a step forward. "Fight it." But there was something in Dante's voice I'd never heard before. Defeat.

Killough's arms shook, the mace quivering. His arms rose above Quincy's chest. "Do it!" he yelled at Dante. And with an anguished cry, he plunged the weapon at Quincy's heart.

Dante kicked the vampire, knocking his blow off line. The iron-studded ball smashed the tile next to Quincy. "I'm sorry." Dante locked eyes with Killough, and the man nodded even as the soul inside him raised the mace for another attack. Dante brought my sword up and swung it like a baseball bat.

The cut wasn't clean, but it served its grotesque purpose. Killough's head toppled from his body and rolled in a lopsided path across the room.

I didn't have time to comfort Dante. Didn't have time to help Quincy off the floor. Dak stomped towards me, knocking witches out of his way, his intent clear.

His skin looked worse than it usually did. Cut in places, burnt in others. Bane had damaged him. But Bane was nowhere to be seen.

And Dak was still standing.

My rage started low in my belly. It gathered, grew larger, hotter, with every step I took toward the demon. We were practically running at each other by the time we clashed. I flew into him, digging my fingernails into his chest as I slammed my forehead into his face.

Without a nose to break, there was no satisfying crunch. It probably hurt my head more than it did his, but Dak did fall back a step. From my perch clinging to his chest, I had a much better view of the room.

Gareth was trading spell after spell with Lucifer.

Dante was taking on the remaining warlock from the black lodge.

And I still didn't see Bane.

The fire in my belly grew larger, took over my whole body. A voice deeper than my usual one spoke. "You're going to die today, demon. Painfully." He'd touched my professor. He was going to pay.

He blinked. And the smallest hint of fear swirled in his eyes.

My inner bitch was just that scary.

He grabbed the back of my shirt and threw me off of him.

I spun, centered myself, and landed on my feet like a cat. I charged back at him. Energy poured from my hands, lashing into him and throwing him on his back. I jumped and landed on his chest.

He sent a spell at me. My mind slowed, saw the stream of energy in every sparkling detail, and batted it aside as easily as if it were a pillow. I pinned him to the ground with my magic, then took great pleasure out of pounding my fist into his face, over and over.

Ophelia tumbled to the ground next to us. She jumped to her feet and blasted her attacker with a freezing spell. She gave me a sour look. "Will you stop playing around and finish him?"

I looked at her, back to the tasty morsel beneath me. I shook my head. No, I wanted to play some more.

Three demons stalked toward Ophelia. She set her shoulders and shot spells at them. One demon got through her wall and kept charging.

I sighed, and flicked him away. She was right. There was more fighting to be done. I clambered off Dak and let him stand. "Will you renounce your allegiance to Lucifer?" I asked.

He wiped blood from his eyes. With a bellow, he came at me again.

The spell I hit him with this time wasn't for play. It tore through his skin, flaying him alive.

His scream shook the castle. Fighting stopped as everyone turned to watch his flesh peel from his body. His muscles and internal organs went next until nothing remained but bone. His skeleton fell to the floor, ringing hollowly against the tile.

"Holy shit," Ophelia murmured.

"Dak!" Lucifer tightened his grip around Gareth's neck. His gaze found me, and my inner bitch decided to call it a day. She scuttled away in fear, leaving me alone to face the devil's wrath.

"He was my most valuable servant," Lucifer said. "You will pay for that, little one."

"Put Gareth down and bring it, bitch." I managed to keep my voice firm and my breathing steady,

But it was damn hard.

Gareth narrowed his eyes at me and scowled. He threw a knee into his father's abdomen and dropped to a squat when Lucifer released him. He back-rolled into a standing position. "You will not touch her."

A lick of fire raced over my shoulder. Gasping, I tamped out the flame and clutched my arm to my chest.

Lucifer shrugged. "Touched her."

Gareth roared, charging. Lucifer flipped him over his back then dropped behind him, wrapping his arm around his throat in a chokehold. "You're going to watch as I squeeze the life from him," he said to me. "Then I'll come for you."

"Gareth!" I flung up my hands, feeling the energy coil inside of me. "Apparate." And I pulled the heavy stone blocks from the wall behind them and flung them down on Lucifer.

Gareth blinked into existence on top of the rubble. "Where is he?" He peered under the stones.

Laughter echoed throughout the room. "Nice try, little one. But you forget, I can apparate, too."

The room shook, and I stepped back, unsteady.

"Delaney!" Dante fought his way toward me, worry in every line of his face.

Yeah, I could tell Lucifer was coming for me, too. I just didn't know from which direction.

"Bye, bye, Chosen One." Lucifer waved at me just as he stepped through the portal.

And right as the ceiling came crashing down toward me.

"Look out!" Two small hands pushed me, knocking me to the ground.

I threw up a shield. It was quick and dirty and not overly effective, but it was good enough to block the dust and debris that showered me. It wouldn't have done much against the hundred-pound chunks of stone that landed beside me, however.

Dante knelt next to me. "Are you okay?"

I nodded and let Gareth pull me to my feet. "Yeah." The portal shimmered then disappeared. The demons and witches that could, blinked out of the room, leaving us with just the dead and injured.

Bane shouldered his way through the crowd, his face tight.

My knees went weak, and Gareth tightened his grip on my arm.

Bane was alive. Bloody and with gunk in his hair I didn't want to identify, but alive.

And we'd just had our asses handed to us. I glanced around the room. It wasn't just Lucifer's people who were injured and dead. Many of our forces were down, too. But Hazel and Quincy looked relatively unharmed. All three of my men were alive. And...

I looked back to where Ophelia and I had just been standing. It was empty except for the large pile of rubble. The boulders that someone had saved me from.

"Oh sweet Jesus," I breathed. Then I dove onto the rocks and started digging.

Chapter Twenty

The linoleum-tiled hallways didn't change, but I kept turning the corners hoping to see something different. Wishing I could be anywhere but here.

She was alive.

It had taken all of Bane's skills to keep Ophelia that way until we'd gotten her to the magical hospital in New York, but she was alive and in surgery and would come out of this her normal, bitchy self.

I stopped and leaned against a pastel-pink wall. She'd looked so small when we'd dug her out. Small and mangled and innocent. There had been so much blood. And, God, her leg...

I shook off that image and resumed my march around the corridors. I had to think of the big picture, not of one individual soldier. But the big picture sucked. There had been three other deaths in our group besides Killough, three witches I didn't know. Bane said we were lucky that our losses were so small.

I didn't feel lucky. I felt like a fraud. Everyone had expected the fucking Chosen One to lead them to victory. All I'd led them to was pain and defeat.

Hazel fell into step on my right, Quincy on my left. They matched my long strides but said nothing. They just kept me company.

"How's your mom?" I asked Hazel. I'd found out that when Bane had disappeared, he'd gone to help Mrs. Willowtree with a nasty wound on her shoulder.

"In pain. Groggy. Pissed off." Hazel shoved her hair behind her ear. "She has to rest for a couple of days. I don't want her in any more battles."

We passed the nurses' station. The witch behind the counter smiled up at me with sympathy.

I didn't want it. "Understood," I told Hazel. "It's not like we have anything planned anyway." Which had been stupid. As a leader, I should have planned for all contingencies. Should have thought about how we would move forward if we'd lost.

But I hadn't thought we would lose. Yes, rationally, I'd known that was an option. But deep down, I hadn't felt it. I hadn't imagined that all of us working together could ever fail.

Hazel grabbed my arm, pulling me to a stop. "I'm going home to be with my family. Quince, too." She jutted her chin at him. "But you'll call us as soon as you come up with a plan. As soon as you need us to fight, we'll be there."

I don't know why that was what did me in, but it was. My shoulders curved in on themselves. Fat tears escaped my eyes. I buried my face in my hands and sobbed.

"Um..." Quincy patted my back. "What do we do?" he whispered to Hazel.

Hazel threw her arms around me. "Hug her, you idiot."

Carefully, Quincy wrapped both of us up in his embrace. I lost track of how long we stood there, me crying and my friends holding me, but that's how Bane found us.

He cleared his throat. "The surgeon is in the waiting room. There's news." He pulled a handkerchief from his pocket and handed it to me.

He'd cleaned up and changed after his wounds had been treated, and forced me to do the same. He was back in his tweed blazer with the elbow patches, and something about those little ovals of suede made my heart squeeze. They were so normal. A part of yesterday's world of homework assignments and fantasizing about being naughty for the professor.

I blew my nose into the linen and shoved it in my back pocket.

This was my new normal. I had to get used to it. "Let's go."

The waiting room was small. It only held fifteen or so chairs. Mr. and Mrs. Ravencroft, Ophelia's parents, sat huddled together, a doctor kneeling in front of them, speaking quietly. Gareth sat in the corner, arms crossed over his chest, his face as hard as stone. Dante stood by the window, looking like he'd rather jump through it than be here.

I waited by the door, not wanting to intrude on the Ravencrofts.

"I'll be back," Bane murmured, and went to sit on Mrs. Ravencroft's other side. He nodded at something the doctor said. When Mrs. Ravencroft's face crumbled, he squeezed her hand as her husband pressed her cheek into his chest.

I nodded numbly to the doctor as he left the room. Waited with ice in my veins as Bane rose and came toward us.

"She'll survive," he said. "She has multiple internal injuries, fractured vertebra, but she's stable and she'll recover."

I looked to Ophelia's sobbing mother. "And?"

Bane's nostrils flared. "They had to take her leg."

Hazel gasped. Quincy looked sick. I merely nodded. Thirty seconds ago, I'd thought she was dead. That that was why her mom was crying. A missing limb we could work with. We could work with anything as long as she lived.

I bobbed my head at the Ravencrofts. "Her parents? Do they need any help to stay here? A hotel? Clothes?"

Bane gave me a faint smile. "It's been taken care of."

Hazel hugged me again. "Our parents are leaving soon. We're going to head out with them."

"Of course." I kissed Quincy's cheek. "Take care of yourselves."

I steeled myself as I watched them walk away. Nodded stoically as Ophelia's parents left. I closed the door and faced my men. "So. What's next?"

Gareth glared at his boots.

Dante turned from the window. His eyes looked as hollow as I felt. "We lost. Is there a next?"

I frowned. "There has to be something next." I looked between them. "Right?"

"Another chance to get our asses kicked, maybe." Gareth slammed the side of his fist into the wall, punching a hole through the sheetrock.

Dante rubbed his temple. "I hate to agree with him, but I don't know how to defeat Lucifer. He's too powerful. Unless the upper world decides to join the battle?" He arched an eyebrow at Bane.

Bane sighed. "They aren't interested. A witch from your lodge is trying to negotiate with the archangels. She thought with the additional information that Lucifer is behind the trouble that it might bring some of them to their senses. But," he said, spreading his hands, "they don't care much about middle world. They don't care about anything except their own cushy existences. Unless Lucifer threatens that, we're on our own."

"Do they really think he'll stop at middle world?" I hadn't listened to much in history class, but even I knew that no authoritarian ever stopped at one conquest. The desire for power was always expanding, until it ran up against a hard wall.

I'd hoped we'd be that wall.

Bane shrugged. "Angels can be particularly difficult to reason with."

I tapped my fingers against my thigh. "I'm hearing a lot of things we can't do. I want to hear some options about what we *can* do." I pointed at Gareth. "Go."

He slouched deeper into the chair. "Why are you asking me? I was unable to defeat my father. I'm useless."

I huffed out a deep breath. Pity parties were never attractive, but it looked particularly pathetic on a big, brooding demon.

I nodded to Dante. "What about you?"

He stared at his hands. "I don't know. Tell me what to do and I'll do it. But there are some things we can't change." He turned back to look out the window. "Lives have been ended. Perhaps it's the end for us, too."

"Great." Another defeatist. Dante had shit tons of guilt weighing him down, so I tried not to hold his attitude against him. But, damn, would it come down to me and Bane rallying the troops? Bane wasn't the cheerleader type, and I'd probably lost any goodwill I had with the other witches.

Thank God, Bane was the organizer in our group. He'd have something. I gave him an encouraging smile.

He laced his fingers together behind his head and closed his eyes.

I waited, hoping each second of silence was another brilliant part of a plan clicking into place.

He opened his eyes, his piercing blue gaze lasering into me. “I’m sorry, Delaney. I fear we’ve lost everything.”

Chapter Twenty-One

A baby dragon. That cloud definitely looked like a baby dragon with two tiny puffs of smoke coming out of its nostrils.

I lay on my back, partially covered by the shade of a large oak tree on Raven grounds. It had been three days since the battle. Three days of stony silence from Gareth, of sleepless nights trying to comfort Dante as he tossed and turned, of hopeless conversations. Bane and I exceled at those.

A bee landed on my bare leg. I watched it, waiting to see if it would sting, not really caring either way. I flexed my right foot. What would it be like to wake up and find that my leg was gone? How had Ophelia dealt with that unbelievable shock? I should visit her in the hospital, but something told me she wouldn't want me to see her, not now. Maybe not ever.

Someone lay down beside me.

I turned my head. Dante stared up at my dragon. His scruff had grown out to a full-on beard. Lines etched the corners of his red eyes.

"You drew the short straw today, huh?" The bee left my leg looking for sweeter pastures.

"What do you mean?"

"You pulled guard duty," I told him. "It hasn't escaped my notice that I've barely been left alone. You guys are worried that Lucifer will come for me." Or in Bane's case, that I might go to Lucifer. Since I hadn't saved the world, he must be wondering if I'd take the other route. Become Lucifer's bitch or whatever it was that went through Bane's head. "You guys used to want to spend time with me, but now it seems like it's a duty."

"You're not a duty, Delaney."

"Then how come none of you have looked me in the eyes for the past three days?" I made my voice light, but inside, I hurt. The academy was empty except for us four, everyone else having gone home to lick their wounds. My men were all I had, but it sometimes felt like they were ghosts, wandering past me but never truly interacting.

We'd lost, but I hadn't thought that would mean I'd lose them, too.

Dante turned his head, his gaze hot. "We let you down. We're ashamed."

"What?" I rolled up onto one elbow. "That's the stupidest thing I've heard. How the hell did you let me down?"

He went back to staring at the sky. "We were useless. Gareth is not only pissed that he couldn't beat his father, but that he was taken by surprise. He thought Dak was the leader. Lucifer played him. Bane's angry because he didn't defeat Dak, and it sure doesn't help his ego that you blew through that monster's defenses and killed him. And I..."

"You saved Quincy," I said fiercely. "It's what Killough wanted you to do."

He slid his hand across the grass and tangled his fingers with mine. "I know that. I *know* it. But it doesn't stop it from hurting. I shouldn't have let him come to the castle. We knew Lucifer had recruited souls. I should have made him sit it out."

I huffed. "Did Killough take orders from you? He was his own man. Made his own decisions." I squeezed his hand. "We've all made our choices. And you need to know, if something happens to me, I would choose it all again. Being a witch, coming to Raven, even that stupid prophecy. I'd want it all. Because it brought me to you guys."

He opened his mouth, and I pressed my finger to his lips. "I know, nothing's going to happen to me." Dante couldn't let himself believe otherwise.

He pulled me across his chest and brought my head down. The kiss said everything our words couldn't. It was love and comfort. Worry and support. We didn't take it any farther; we didn't need to.

I rested my head on his chest and enjoyed the slight rise and fall from his breathing. The heat of the sun on my back. The connection I only felt when I was with Dante or Gareth or Bane.

"'*She who is born to the witch who comes this year will be the alpha and the omega.*'" The first line of the prophecy slid softly off my tongue. Was there something we'd missed in the oracle's words? I'd gone over it a million times, but still I hoped for new inspiration.

"'*She will be the bringer of peace, and the advance guard of war,*'" Dante said.

"'*Many magical creatures will die in the battle.*'" That was the part I hated most.

"'*That which saves us will also destroy.*'"

"'*That which destroys, can also be destroyed.*'" A shiver raced down my spine, and Dante hugged me tighter.

"'*She has the power to end our world.*'"

We spoke the last line together. "*Quidquid id est, timeo de ignotis.*'"

"Whatever it is, I fear the unknown," I translated. But I didn't. The prophecy might be about me, but that last part didn't fit. Somewhere these past three days, my fear had left me.

I was mortal. I was going to die. I hoped I'd have more time. More time to develop my abilities, to see the world, to learn each and every inch of all of my men. But if it wasn't to be, I was still fortunate in everything I had done and seen in my life. Lucky to love the three greatest men I'd ever known.

"Any new inspiration strike you?" Dante asked.

"Nope." I scratched my fingers through his beard. I think I liked him better this way. He was like a sexy mountain man.

"And the second prophecy Hedwig told you?"

I sighed. "'*With the power of four, there will be magic enough to end the war. With the power of four, the world will be changed forevermore.*'" There were four of us. Even though Bane didn't want to make our relationship intimate, he couldn't deny we were all a unit. And we were definitely stronger together, but as our ass-kicking had shown, the four of us fighting together hadn't—

I pushed up, my hand pressing into Dante's chest, making him wheeze. "What if it's not about fighting?"

Dante set me to the side. He sat up and took in a full breath. "What?"

I jumped to my feet and paced around the tree. "It could make sense." My mind raced over the prophecies again. Then flew to the chants I heard in my weird dreams. My cheeks heated as I remembered those dreams. In some, my men would repeat the prophecy, usually while making my body burn.

Sometimes the dreams ended with them trying to kill me.

Like I said, they were farkin' weird. That's how dreams worked. But there had been another one, a dream where three faceless men took turns pleasuring me.

I rapped my knuckles into my palm. What were the exact words? *When three makes one, blessed be. Your doubting heart will call to flee. But when Strength, Determination, and Loyalty decree. Rejoice, little one, for you shall be free.*

"That's it." I grabbed Dante's hand and pulled him to standing. "We have to go."

"Go where?"

I flashed him a grin. "Somewhere where I can impress you all with my brilliance. I have an idea." It was bat-shit crazy and completely self-serving, but it was a plan. And since we'd been wandering around for the past three days doing nothing but navel-gazing, any plan was an improvement.

Dante gave me the side-eye. "Every time you smile like that, I get a little worried."

"Don't be worried," I said. "This time, you should be scared out of your damn mind."

Chapter Twenty-Two

"Why did Lucifer leave the castle?" I asked. "Why not finish us off when he had the chance?" We were in Dante's room, Bane, Gareth, and Dante sitting on his sofa and chairs with me pacing before them.

"He'd made his point," Bane said.

Dante shrugged. "Maybe he had some other witches to squash under his thumb waiting for him."

Gareth said nothing, just flexed and unflexed his hands.

I kicked his leg. "Hey. Enough with the pity party. It's time to get back in the game."

He raised his head. "We can't defeat Lucifer. It's over."

I shook my head. Pathetic. All of them. I resumed my pacing. "We need to try at least one more thing."

"There is nothing else," Gareth insisted.

I fisted my hands on my hips. "There's always one more thing to try. Now, if you were going to think like optimists and not like the big, whiny babies you actually are, what would be some reasons Lucifer left?"

Bane shifted on the sofa. He ran his hand through his hair and sighed. "Right. He wasn't feeling assured of a victory?"

I nodded. "Good, but let's make these sound less like questions and more like definitive statements." I bobbed on my feet, feeling a rush of energy. This was the easy part. Convincing them of my plan was where I'd run into trouble.

Dante pursed his lips. "You had just killed Dak. It might have scared him."

I batted my hand through the air. "It was a battle. He had to know some of his minions would die."

"No." Bane shook his head. "Dante's right. Dak was powerful. He had magical wards raised and you blew right through them. Lucifer would have to take notice of that kind of power."

I looked at Gareth. "You know him better than anyone. Could Lucifer be scared of us?"

Gareth cracked a knuckle. "No. Not scared. But..." He straightened form his slouch in the armchair. "Perhaps he is wary."

"Wary. I'll take it." I pulled my phone from my back pocket and tossed it to Bane. "Even if Lucifer were scared, I wouldn't want to go head-to-head with him. We might defeat him, but how many on our side would die in the battle? I want to fight smarter."

"And your phone will help?" Bane held it up. "What's your code?"

"Three two four three." My cheeks warmed. "The first letter of all our names as they show up on the keypad in the order of when I met you." I cleared my throat. "Go to my texts with Hazel."

He drew his brows together. "This appears to be research on the Root of Corruption. How is this relevant?"

"No." Gareth growled. "That's a foolish plan."

"Huh." I crossed my arms over my chest. "I really thought Bane would be the first to figure it out." But it made sense; Gareth and I did tend to think alike when it came to fights.

"Hey." Dante frowned. "What the hell?"

"Have you figured her plan out yet?" Gareth asked.

Dante slouched in his seat.

Bane thumbed off my phone and tossed it back. "It would be difficult enough to get Lucifer's blood into the Root, but obtaining the artifact is near impossible. No one has succeeded."

"And that's where my plan comes in." I sat on the edge of the coffee table and looked each of my men in their eyes. "As Hazel pointed out, the problem is that only one person can enter the In-Between to get the Root. And no one person seems powerful enough to survive. But what if we combined our powers, if I was able to take them with me when I took the shamanic journey?" That was something else Hazel had learned. Travelling to the In-Between wasn't exactly like shamanic travels, but it was close enough to help me understand what it was going to be like when I got there.

"It wouldn't be you taking the journey." Bane rubbed his jaw. "I'll go, but tell me what you're thinking."

I laughed. "Sorry, for my plan to work, I'm really the only option." I chewed on my bottom lip then decided to just blurt it out. Nothing would be gained by soft-pedaling it. "I think we should use sex magic to lend me some of your powers before I journey to the In-Between."

Dead silence met my announcement. And darkness, but that might be because I'd screwed my eyes shut. I peeled one open to gauge their reactions.

They didn't look encouraging.

"All the signs point toward this." I leaned forward, pressing my elbows to my knees. "Druella's second prophecy is about the power of four." I swirled my finger in the air, indicating all of us. "We're the four, and we need to leverage our powers. I don't think it's a coincidence that I have a relationship with each of you." I pointed at Bane. "I know we haven't consummated it, but you can't deny there's something between us. Christ, my dreams even say this is the answer."

When three makes one, blessed be.

I had to believe that referred to my three men, especially as it was whispered in my ear during the hottest sex dream I'd ever had. When three of my lovers came together as one, in one freaky, hot ménage.

My nipples tingled. My plan was serious business. It was to save the world and all that. But I couldn't deny the thrill that shot through me at the thought of going forward with it. Of having each of my guys touch me at the same time. Of—

"Absolutely not." Bane stood. "That is off the table."

I jumped to my feet. "Do you have any other ideas?"

He pressed his lips together.

"I could hide you away," Gareth offered. "There are places in the lower world even Lucifer can't find."

"What exactly would we do in exile?" Did they have Netflix in lower world?

Gareth shrugged. "We can learn how to make sourdough bread. We'll be happy."

"A gilded prison. No thanks." Although sourdough toast did sound tasty right about now. Ignoring my stomach, I poked Bane's chest. "And you? Is this when you launch your plan to eliminate the Chosen One? Are you willing to kill me but not fuck me?"

He blanched.

It was a low blow, I'll admit. But a girl's ego could only take so much, and I was getting tired of him treating me like I was a leper. Unless...

The back of my throat burned. "If you really don't want to have sex with me, then we'll come up with something else." I included all of them in my gaze. "I don't want to force this on anyone. No one can feel like it's a sacrifice." Because even to save the world, there were some things I just wouldn't do. Like force someone to have sex.

"It's no hardship fucking you, pet." Gareth twined a strand of my hair around his finger. "But I don't want you going to the In-Between alone."

I cupped his hand. "If my plan works, I wouldn't be going alone. I'd be taking a part of each of you with me. But if anyone else has another idea?" I looked around hopefully, like someone had a magic button he could press to make Lucifer disappear.

No one did. "Then I say we go with the one plan we have. Use sex magic to get me through the In-Between alive and get the Root, use it on Lucifer, and save the world." I nodded. It definitely had a fiftyish percent chance of succeeding.

Bane closed his eyes. "Every part of that plan is supremely improbable."

"The Chosen One's power combined with that of her chosen mates?" I infused my voice with as much optimism as I could. "That combination will be unstoppable."

It had to be.

Chapter Twenty-Three

Bane had shaken his head when I'd exited Dante's bathroom in my nubby, terry cloth robe. He'd created a portal, disappeared into his room, and returned with a deep blue silk one that fell to my ankles.

It might have had a masculine cut, but it felt like heaven against my bare skin, smelled of Bane, and made me feel sexy as hell.

Which was good, because I needed all the sexy juju I could get.

I fiddled with the belt. "Um, I know this was my idea, but it feels weird. Clinical."

Dante had the biggest bed, so we'd stayed in his room. Bane had drilled me for hours about what was known of the In-Between's defenses, gone over every excruciating aspect of the spell we'd used to join our powers, until I was ready to join Lucifer's side just to escape the conversation.

The idea of making love to all three of my men at the same time was awesome.

The execution of it not so much. Bane was choreographing every moment. I had been an idiot to ever think this would be sexy.

Bane examined his notes. "We're performing a high-level spell. It is clinical."

Dante elbowed him. "Ass." He turned his full-wattage smile on me. "Relax. This will be good. We'll have you so primed and focused, nothing will be able to stop you in the In-Between."

Gareth gripped my wrist and yanked me into his body. He spun, pinning me against the wall.

A small 'eek' slipped past my lips, but my body curved to his automatically.

"Do you doubt me, pet?" He ran his nose along my throat, inhaling deeply. "Doubt that I'll make this good? Your body knows the pleasure I can bring it. I'll have you so wrung out from ecstasy it won't matter the other two will fail to compare. You'll be so overwrought, their pitiful attempts at lovemaking will come as a much-needed respite."

I smiled even as my body hummed from his nearness. With a new plan in place, my demon's sulk had disappeared. He was fully focused, fully committed, and that promised only good things for me.

"Did I ever tell you that I find your insecurities adorable?" I said.

He growled, picked me up by the hips, and tossed me a good five feet to Dante's bed.

I bounced on the mattress and shoved a hank of hair out of my face. "It was a joke."

"I know." He prowled toward the bed, stripping off his clothes as he went. "But now is not the time for humor."

He crawled over me, his tattoos swirling like crazy. His knees pinned my thighs, his large hands caging my head. He had me trapped just where I wanted to be, and the predatory gleam in his gold eyes turned my insides liquid.

"Oh my," I whispered.

"Oh, we're starting now, are we?"

I turned my head to glare at Bane, The Mood Killer, as he'd henceforth be known.

Gareth pinched my chin and turned me back to face him. "Forget him. Forget everything but me, and how I make you feel." He kissed the hollow between my breasts as he untied my belt. He unfolded one side of the robe, then the other. Cool air kissed my breasts.

Then Gareth did.

I slid my eyes shut and arched into his touch. His mouth was hot, wet, around my nipple, and arcs of pleasure streaked through me. The awkwardness of the situation melted away until it was only me and Gareth, doing what we did best together.

The bed sank on my right side, and Dante's fingers swept through my hair. "You're so hot, baby." He sucked my earlobe into his mouth. "Are you wet, too?"

A hand, his, Gareth's, I didn't know, slid down my side, across my triangle of hair. A finger slipped between my folds and traced a path from my clit to my opening.

"Mmm." Dante hummed. "So wet. I can't wait to taste you."

Gareth grunted. "Me first." He licked his way down my body, shouldering my thighs wide. He ghosted a breath across my lower lips, and I whimpered. He waited, his lips inches from my body, taunting me.

I tried to wriggle closer, force the contact, but four hands held me down. Four hands stroked my skin, plucked at my nipples, drove me mad, until finally, finally, Gareth lowered his head and licked me.

If it wasn't for those four hands, I would have shot off the bed. The feel of his tongue sliding between my folds was electric. Almost too good to take. I grabbed Dante behind his head, digging my fingers into his hair. I needed something to hold onto, and Gareth's shaved head wasn't going to cut it.

Gareth drew a figure eight, rounding my opening, and circling my clit, so tantalizingly close, but never quite touching.

My hips rocked of their own accord. My lungs pulled tight, making it a struggle to breathe. "Please," I begged.

Gareth chuckled, the sound vibrating through my core. "Shall we take pity on her?"

Dante kissed the edge of my mouth. "Seems only fair."

I nodded, my hair scraping against the duvet. It *was* only fair. I was laid out for each of them to take their pleasure in. It was only right that— "Oh God!"

Gareth's lips latched onto my clit the same moment Dante took my nipple in his mouth and sucked.

My eyes flew open. The sight of Gareth between my legs and Dante at my breast was mesmerizing. Beautiful.

But still my gaze left them and searched out the missing member of our group.

Bane stood next to the bed. He set a brass bowl of smoking frankincense down on the side table. His skin was flushed and the zipper of his slacks was tented. He licked his bottom lip, and the sight of his wanting me made me clench.

I stretched out a hand.

After one agonizing moment, he took it. He kissed my palm, then nipped the fleshy part. Keeping his gaze on mine, he stripped out of his jacket, tossing it on the floor. His crisp, white shirt was next, revealing a firm chest, dark hair, and abs that didn't quit.

By the time he was naked, I was panting. He crawled next to me and cupped my cheek, brushing his thumb along my cheekbone. His smile was bittersweet. "You're so damn beautiful."

"Right back at ya," I whispered. Then I raised my head for his kiss.

My mind emptied into a moment of perfect clarity. All three of my men were touching me. Loving me. I could see all four of us, as if my spirit hovered above, looking down. Gareth, fierce and loyal, doing unspeakable things between my legs. Dante, determined to do what was right, to give me everything I needed, loving at my breast. And Bane...

Bane was so strong. So damned ethical. I was going to make sure he didn't regret this. That he woke up tomorrow feeling hope for the future, not repentance for the past.

The tension built within me. My thighs clamped around Gareth. I moaned into Bane's mouth. And gasped in indignation when Gareth stole his lovely tongue away from me, leaving me high and dry.

I glared down my body. "Don't you dare stop."

He rose up to kneeling and hooked my ankles over his shoulders. "Too close. You're coming with me." He notched his crown at my entrance and pressed inside in one smooth stroke.

We moaned in unison.

"Mine," Gareth said. He nipped my calf and spread his hand possessively at the top of my mons.

"Ours," Dante said.

Gareth only grunted, but it sounded like agreement.

Bane's eyes burned with an emotion I couldn't read. He turned my head and took my mouth again, the thrusts of his tongue eerily mirroring Gareth.

I wasn't sure how he felt about sharing. I did know how being shared felt: fan-fucking-tastic.

I placed my palm on Dante's abdomen and slid it lower. I reached the base of his cock and gripped it tightly. He was thick and warm in my hand, and his tortured groan matched how I felt.

Bane drew back and moved lower. He plumped one of my breasts, circling his thumb around my areola. He looked at my body with such wonder it was like he'd never seen boobs before.

I smiled, everything about the moment perfection. Gareth, pistoning in and out of me, sparking every nerve ending in my channel to life. Dante gripping my hand in his, directing my movements, taking his pleasure. And Bane, finally, finally, giving in to our desires.

He kissed the tip of my nipple. "It's time to say your line."

My line? I drew my eyebrows together. Oh. Yeah. There was a reason we were doing this, and it didn't have anything to do with me getting off. But I could hardly make my mouth move. Speaking a line from a spell seemed impossible.

But the words took shape in my head, words I'd written. We'd each come up with a line for the spell. Thank God mine was first because in a few seconds I wouldn't be able to think, much less talk.

I looked to each of my guys. "When bodies join, from mouth to loin." And yes, my line definitely had the lamest rhyme. Writing spells wasn't my forte as a witch.

Gareth plowed deep and held himself inside me. "Our powers meld, our magics swell."

"When our hearts beat as one." Dante ran his thumb along my lips, pressing inside. I suckled on the tip.

Bane locked eyes with me. I think he was trying to block out Dante and Gareth. "All obstacles shall be overcome," he finished.

The air thickened. My skin hummed as if an electric current ran through me. Gareth gripped my hips and increased his pace.

My back arched. It was too good, all of their hands on me. All the love they showed me. In this moment, all our emotions were exposed, nothing was hidden. Yes, we were doing this to defeat Lucifer. And yes, people had sex all the time without affection. But this was different. This was more.

The frankincense smoke filled my nose, thick and sweet, making me light-headed.

My muscles coiled tighter with each of Gareth's thrusts. I grabbed one of Dante's hands, one of Bane's.

Bane kissed the back of my hand, and pressed it to the duvet beside my head, keeping his grip tight.

Dante did the same.

I raised my hips, meeting Gareth as he took me, feeling myself rise to the point of no return.

Bane murmured our spell as I toppled over the peak.

"Yes!" My core clamped around Gareth's cock as my toes curled. Pleasure rocketed through me. Instead of feeling limp and wrung out as I usually did after I orgasmed, I felt renewed. Strong. When Gareth roared and emptied himself inside me, I felt every hot splash of his cum, felt his power joining with mine.

Gareth dug his fingers into my skin before easing back. He kissed the top of my triangle before moving aside.

Dante filled his place.

"The spell," Bane said. "Again."

"When bodies join, from mouth to loin," I said as Dante eased inside me. I took him eagerly, greedily, hardly hearing Gareth as he chanted, "Our powers meld, our magics swell."

Dante bottomed out. A bead of sweat rolled down his temple. "When our hearts beat as one."

"All obstacles shall be overcome," Bane said.

Dante started to move. Gareth lay beside me, taking my mouth in one drugging kiss before Bane turned my head and took over. Every inch of my skin was caressed, worshipped. My magic hummed. My inner bitch even seemed content, like a cat dozing in a patch of sunlight.

I wrapped my legs around Dante's waist, pulling him into me. Wet heat encircled my nipple, and I didn't look to see whose head was at my breast. It didn't matter. The world was getting fuzzy around the edges, my other senses dimming as my body felt every inch of Dante's length, felt every caress, lick, and kiss from my other men. I was one giant nerve, and every touch brought me pleasure.

Bane's voice hummed in my ear. The spell, I realized. He chanted it faster, faster, and my body responded. My lungs squeezed, my walls clamped around Dante's cock, and I was flying. Wave after wave of ecstasy flooded my veins.

His fangs dropped. Dante threw his head back and howled at the ceiling as he came.

My skin prickled with energy. I arched onto my shoulder blades, drawing him deeper, eking out every last pulse as if his cum belonged to me. Because it did. Every part of these men was mine, just like I was theirs. When we joined together, it seemed so simple, so clear. The fates had brought us together. It was up to us not to let anything tear us apart.

I held my breath as Dante crawled to my side and Bane took his place. His cock rose from a thatch of dark hair, long and thick. My mouth watered, I wanted to taste him so badly. After all his dismissals, his rejections, he was finally mine. I ignored the small part of my heart that ached knowing he'd only given in because we needed his magic.

He would have come around eventually, I tried to convince myself. Necessity only sped the process along.

His gaze raked my body, from the hair on my head to the small mole on my upper thigh.

I swallowed, the back of my throat going thick. My worry evaporated. Everything I needed to know was in that look. His need. His acceptance.

His love.

"Say it again," he told me.

And when I repeated my line of the spell this time, it sounded different. Not awkward and stilted. The words were the same, but this time it came out sounding a lot like 'I love you.'

He placed his palms on my inner knees, pressing my thighs wider. Gripping the base of his length, he notched the head at my opening as Gareth and Dante chanted. When it came to Bane's line, he pressed inside as he spoke it.

I closed my eyes, a feeling of perfect bliss enveloping me. Finally, he was mine. They were mine.

Bane plowed deep. "Fuck me," he cursed. "You feel so good. Never want to leave."

I bit my lip and nodded. I wouldn't say no to that.

Dante chuckled. "Just think, you could have had this all these months if you'd pulled that stick out of your ass earlier." He slid his hand over my belly, lower, until the tip of his finger rested against my clit. "It was definitely your loss."

"Sod off." Bane surged into me. He gripped my ass, and lifted me into his thrusts. "So fucking good," he murmured.

Strong hands gripped my wrists, pulled my hands over my head. I opened my eyes to gaze into Gareth's. The gold had gone dark, his pupils looking more like copper. He traced my lips, my cheekbones, the ridge of my nose. "You will be safe, pet," he ordered. "You will come back to us."

"I will." Confidence flooded me. Each stroke increased my power. And need.

Bane fucked me harder. Faster. He began chanting our spell, joined by Gareth and Dante.

My throat closed. I yanked at my hands, but Gareth held me steady. Fire raced beneath my skin. *Please,*

please, please. The word echoed in my head. The room grew brighter, and I gasped, seeing it was my body that glowed.

Their voices rose.

"*When bodies join, from mouth to loin,*

Our powers meld, our magics swell,

When our hearts beat as one,

All obstacles shall be overcome."

I thrashed beneath them. My core clenched tighter, tighter. Dante swirled his finger over my clit, and I was gone.

The bed disappeared beneath me. All I felt was liquid heat pulse from my core outward, engulfing my entire body. The pleasure was so great it bordered on pain.

Through a fog, I heard Bane's spell change. As power rippled through me, he intoned the words that would send me to the In-Between.

"*From north and south, east and west, let the In-Between welcome this guest.*

Turmoil, pain, nor disruption, only let her find the Root of Corruption."

A cord snapped through me, jerking my limbs straight. I fluttered my eyelids, blinked, and drew them wide.

Dante's bedroom had disappeared.

I was in the In-Between.

Chapter Twenty-Four

The In-Between wasn't dark, wasn't light. A sort of even grayness was all that filled my vision. There was no sound except that of my own breathing. It echoed back at me, like I was in a small room or closet.

"Hello?" I felt for my legs. Relief coursed through me when I discovered I had a body. I hadn't been sure. I felt floaty and insubstantial.

It could have been the after-effects of all those orgasms.

I stood, and took a step forward, hands outstretched. "Can anyone hear me?" Or anything. If Bane's spell had worked, I should be where the Root of Corruption was located. But the In-Between was a tricky place. According to a book Hazel had read, there was no space where it should be able to exist; but it did. Hazel guessed it was another dimension, one where physical distance had no meaning.

I waved my hand in front of my face, trying to dispel some of the mist. Was it lighter to my left? I turned and eased my way in that direction. It took me longer than it should have. Not being able to see well, I made sure there was something solid beneath my foot before putting my weight on it. I didn't care if I looked like an idiot. I was in another dimension and didn't know what the rules were. I didn't want to fall into nothingness.

"Another one has come." A hooded figure shimmered to my right.

"It has been awhile." Another one spoke to my left.

It was the black lodge, and I was back in the castle outside Ottawa. The witches we'd fought were the guardians of the Root. Bane had told me figures in the In-Between might take the appearance of those I knew, but seeing it still made my hair stand on end.

I cleared my throat. "I've come for the Root of Corruption. If you'll just point me in the right direction, I'll be on my way. Please."

One of the figures leaned forward, its hood slipping. Its face lay in shadow, and something told me I was lucky I couldn't see clearly. Things moved on the dark oval that shouldn't be moving.

"If you tell a lie, we will hang you." A platform with a noose appeared behind him.

Another figure said, "And if you tell the truth, we will cut off your head." A long sword appeared in its hands, the blade digging into the ground.

"Now, what say you?" asked a third figure.

"Uh, wut?" What the hell was this? Apparently they didn't want me to talk. Should I just start fighting?

I centered myself, reached deep into my core.

And felt nothing.

"Magic is not allowed in the In-Between."

Perfect. Just flippin' perfect. If I couldn't use magic, and I really didn't think they expected me to just start beating heads, then that left using my brain.

Not my strong suit.

I inhaled deeply and ran the words through my head. It was a riddle, but one I thought would come with real consequences if I got it wrong. I eyed the noose. The sword. Neither death seemed more appealing than the other.

I paced back and forth. Think, damn it. If I couldn't tell the truth or a lie, what was left to say. Bane would have known. He'd—

I paused. I couldn't use magic here, but a spell had already been cast. Now I just had to access it.

I closed my eyes, examining how I felt.

Strong. Power did course through me, and it didn't only belong to myself. Each of my men had lent me some of their own essence. Would it be enough to save me?

I thought about Bane, imagining every inch of him before me. The confident tilt of his chin. His delicious lips. His piercing eyes. I stared into those imaginary eyes, falling deeper and deeper. Energy rippled up my spine, and right into my brain.

My eyes snapped open. "You will hang me," I said confidently, knowing that wasn't going to happen.

The hoods swiveled toward each other, disapproving clicking sounds echoing through the room.

"That's right, right?" I crossed my arms over my chest. "If I lied, then you would hang me, making my words not a lie. If what I said was the truth, then you'd have to take my head instead of hanging me, which would then make the words a lie. So you can't hang me. It's a little knot you tied for yourselves."

I rolled up onto my toes, rather pleased with myself. If only I could keep Bane's brains with me all the time.

"That is correct." One dark hood nodded.

"The Grim Reaper has 500 crypts," a warlock said. "There are 500 witches who need them. The Reaper asks the first witch to go to every crypt and open it. He tells the second witch to go to every second crypt and close it. The third witch goes to every third crypt, either opening the door or closing it depending on how she finds it. And so on. How many crypts remain open?"

Shit. My stomach sank. Now I had to do math? And creepy math at that.

But Bane taught Arithmancy, and that was mathy. I blew out a breath and closed my eyes, visualizing Bane again. That same surge of power fired my neurons. Numbers rearranged themselves in my mind, falling into place.

I punched my fist into the air. This sex magic shit was the bomb. If the four of us kept it up, I would be unstoppable.

And also very, very satisfied.

"Assuming this isn't a trick question," I said, "since anyone who needs a crypt would be dead and can't open or close anything, then the answer is 22. Something about perfect squares and odd numbers of multipliers."

Imaginary Bane huffed in my mind. *Only perfect squares have an odd number of multipliers. If the crypt door is to be open at the end, it will need an odd number of said multipliers. Three, for example. Open, close, open. Since there are only 22 perfect squares found between one a nd—*

Borrrriinng. Even when he was in my head, I could tune Bane out when he got on one of his lectures.

The shoulders under one black robe sagged. The witch slid a flaming athame back up her sleeve. "Very well. You're smarter than you look, we'll give you that."

I narrowed my eyes.

"The third and final challenge," she continued, "will call on you to use your brawn instead of your brain. Defeat your opponent, and the Root of Corruption shall be yours."

A fight? I danced a little jig. Now this was up my alley, especially with my men's powers racing through me. I felt like Iron Man. Undefeatable.

The mists to my right coalesced, formed a dark shape.

My feet slowed. Stopped. No. It couldn't be.

"If you kill him, the Root will be yours." The black-robed figure settled into her chair. "Begin."

The demon stepped toward me, his golden eyes glowing.

I fell back a step. "Gareth?"

He didn't answer, only took another step. A katana appeared in his hand.

Oh God. I needed another math question. If only this last challenge made me figure out how many numbers between 1 and 500 had perfect squares. That had been a piece of cake compared to this.

A sturdy shaft filled my right hand. I looked down. A battle axe. My snort-laugh came out a tad hysterical. The In-Between got every detail right, down to my favorite weapon.

And my greatest weakness.

"Gareth, what are you doing? Are you spelled?"

He swung at me, and I brought my axe up to block the strike. The clash of metal against metal hurt my ears.

Or maybe it was my heart that hurt.

I ducked another swing. "Gareth, wake up. I can't fight you."

"You choose to forfeit?" A warlock leaned forward eagerly.

I darted under Gareth's arm to the side of the room. My chest heaved. A forfeit while trying for the Root of Corruption was the same as a loss. And a loss meant my death. If I didn't leave the In-Between with the damn artifact in my hand, I wasn't leaving it at all.

"No," I shouted. "No forfeit." I just needed time to think. Time to wake Gareth up from his fugue state. Maybe we could work together and kill—

He didn't give me that time. He charged forward.

I deflected his blade, but his body crashed into mine, sending me flying. I hit the ground hard, my teeth jarring. Using my momentum, I rolled backwards and to my feet, just in time to side-step his next attack.

Gareth turned. His eyes had darkened and there was zero recognition in them. A large tattoo covered his chest, a cross encircled by two thick lines.

Unmoving lines.

I only had a second to ponder that before Gareth hefted his sword in a one-handed grip, and threw it at me like a javelin.

I squawked and bobbed left. A cool breeze caressed my cheek as the blade whooshed past. A hank of violet hair dropped to the floor beside me.

I picked up my fallen ponytail and glared at the fake Gareth. "That," I said, ice filling my voice, "was a step too far." But the near brush with death had cleared my head. Nothing was real in the In-Between. Those weren't the actual witches and warlocks of the black lodge sitting around us, and this wasn't my Gareth. Whatever magic made this world had gotten almost every detail perfect, but it couldn't replicate the magic of Gareth's tattoos. They told his life story, and only he could create it.

An awareness of Gareth, the real Gareth, coiled inside of me, filling my blood. My muscles. *Take no prisoners. Fight to win.* I hefted my axe, feeling a surge of power, of Gareth's fighting prowess. I didn't have the privilege of squeamishness, not anymore. Fake Gareth had to go.

The In-Between replica of my man was good. He had all the strength and skill of the real Gareth.

But he couldn't stand up to me combined with my demon's fierceness. It took thirty seconds before I had my opening. He put his weight on his back leg, and I swept it, bringing him to his knees. I brought the axe up and around my head. And paused.

It was Gareth's neck that was my target. His gold eyes that stared up at me.

A wave of dizziness crashed over me. Something about those gold eyes... They were familiar, of course, but there was something more. Something yet to come.

Do it now, pet, or I will turn you over my knee when you get back.

My head cleared. I swung, smiling grimly. My Gareth was waiting for me, depending on me to get the job done.

Fake Gareth raised his hands, but it was too late. The axe sliced cleanly through his neck, separating his head from his body. He collapsed to the floor, then disappeared.

I plunked the head of the axe on the ground and rested my weight on the handle. I sucked in deep breaths, trying to calm my racing heart. It hadn't been him; I knew that.

But it had still been hard to make that cut.

"She passed," a witch said. "How interesting."

The three figures pushed their hoods back. Bane, Dante, and Gareth stared back at me.

"The Root of Corruption is yours," Bane said. He raised his hand and pointed to the center of the room.

A high table flickered to being, a golden chalice resting on top.

I crept toward it, expecting another 'challenge' to pop up to stop me. Nothing did. I picked up the Root of Corruption and nothing struck me down. My shoulders lowered. The metal was cool beneath my palms, the delicate scrollwork engraved into the metal a slight scratch against my skin.

The artifact looked like a footed bowl – like something I'd want to fill with candy and put on my table. Well, honestly, I'd fill anything with candy, an old shoe even, because, candy. But it definitely looked like something someone's sweet granny would put on her coffee table.

And I was going to use it to destroy the devil.

I nodded to my men's mirror images. "Thanks." I looked around. Waited. But the four of us remained in the In-Between.

"Um, how do I get back?" I asked fake Bane. "Click my heels three times and say 'there's no place like home?'"

Even fake Bane didn't find my snark amusing. He just arched an eyebrow and remained silent.

"Hell." I clutched the chalice to my stomach. It couldn't hurt to try. "There's no place like home," I said each time I tapped my heels together.

Unsurprisingly, it didn't work. I blinked. Well, if—

I blinked again. Three beloved faces hovered above mine, each wearing expressions of concern and relief.

"She's back." Bane blew out a breath, his shoulders sagging. "And she has the artifact." He took the Root from my limp grasp and examined it.

Dante pulled me up to sitting and wrapped his arms around me. We were in his room and on his bed. All of us still naked.

"How long was I gone?"

"Not but a second." Gareth massaged the back of my head.

My eyes flared wide, and I reached up to feel my hair. My body sagged. It was all there. The haircut had stayed in the In-Between. It was like Vegas that way.

"But it felt so much longer," I said. I drank in the sight of my demon, his head firmly intact, then touched each of my men, needing to reassure myself they were really there. "I had to complete three challenges. There's no way all that happened in just an instant."

"Time works differently in the In-Between." Bane set the chalice down. "Some even say it doesn't exist there."

I tried to work that one out, but the sex magic was fading. Bane's brains weren't giving me an inside advantage.

"Are you all right, pet?"

I peeled myself from Dante's arms and nodded. "It was strange, and I don't think I'd want to take a vacay there any time soon, but I'm fine." I looked at the gold cup sitting on the bedside table. "And we have the Root. We're going to do this. We're going to defeat Lucifer."

Bane placed his hand on my knee and squeezed. "Taking on Lucifer will be more challenging than obtaining the chalice."

I shook my head. "Debbie Downer, much?"

His lips twitched. "But, we're one step closer. It is no longer an impossible task."

I held my hand up and tilted it from side to side. "Not great, but you're improving as a cheerleader. I'll take it." I rolled to my knees and pecked Dante's then Gareth's cheeks. I crawled to Bane to give him the same treatment.

He turned his face, meeting my lips with his. The kiss was hard but brief, like he needed to make sure I was real, too.

I sat back on my heels. I became aware of my nakedness and just barely stopped myself from covering my boobs with my arm. The silence in the room became thick. Heavy.

"Was it just for magic?" I wet my lips. I looked at Gareth, with his swirling tattoos and fierce eyes, to Dante, brimming over with love, to Bane. He was still the dark horse. "Or can this continue?" I included all my men in the question even though I was pretty sure about the answers from two of them. "Can we keep what we have between us right here, right now?"

Everyone looked at Bane.

I almost felt bad for him. There was a lot of pressure to give us the right answer.

He narrowed his eyes, the orbs glinting dark blue in the low light. "If we're going to do this, there are going to have to be some changes."

"Oh?" My heart leapt. That didn't sound like a no.

"Though necessary for the spell, I don't think our lovemaking was done in the most efficient manner." He pushed me back onto the bed. Three pairs of eyes snapped to my breasts as they bounced.

Bane crawled over me. He nipped at my bottom lip. "After all, there are three of us, and you have multiple access points. I believe you're going to have to start pulling your weight."

Gareth and Dante lay down on either side of me.

I relaxed back onto the bed. Tomorrow we'd plan, strategize. Then we'd fight, maybe die. But today...

Today, I was the luckiest bitch alive.

"That," I said. "can be arranged."

Chapter Twenty-Five

"Work it again."

I sighed, and slid my finger under my blindfold, scratching an itch. Gareth had mapped out Lucifer's palace, or lair as I liked to call it, LL for short, and had insisted that I practice traveling the corridors with my eyes closed. He and Bane knew I'd peek, however, hence the blindfold.

It was highly annoying that they knew me so well.

"Steady." Dante gripped my arm, earning a curse from Gareth. "There's a rock here," Dante yelled back. "I don't want her to trip."

We were on Raven's soccer field, the only open space on the academy grounds large enough to fit the imaginary dimensions of LL. I'd visualized the crap out of the floorplan until the backs of my eye sockets were imprinted with the map. Gareth swore I'd need to follow the map in my head, and not the hallways of the house once I got there. Apparently, my eyes weren't to be trusted in LL, and people tended to get distracted and lost.

I felt my way past the imaginary ballroom towards the library. I pursed my lips. I couldn't imagine what Gareth would classify as distracting. Prisoners in manacles lining the walls? Demons lashing fallen angels? The gruesome possibilities were endless.

"Tell me the first challenge again." Bane's voice came from over my left shoulder. I knew without looking that he still followed me, pen and pad of paper in hand, documenting everything I could tell him about the In-Between. He wanted to write it all down, for posterity or some shit, and said that the knowledge could help other witches.

I thought it had more to do with satisfying the questions in his secret, nerdy heart then helping witch-kind, but he hadn't appreciated it when I'd expressed that opinion.

I sighed again. It was turning into an annoying habit, but my guys could be damn frustrating. "I already told you. It was that logic puzzle. If I lied, they'd hang me, and if I told the truth, they'd take my head.." I made a sharp left turn, and my shoulder bounced off something warm and firm.

"You clipped the wall there, pet." Gareth nudged me a foot to the right. "But you've remembered the way to Lucifer's study. It's the room he spends the most time in."

"And you figured out the answer?" Bane pressed. "How long were you in the In-Between?"

I planted my hands on my hips. "Hey! What exactly does it say about you if you think your girlfriend is dumb?"

He cupped the back of my neck, rubbing gently at my scalp.

I knew it was Bane's hand. Each man touched me differently.

"I don't think you're stupid. Quite the contrary." Bane scratched me like a cat, and my stupid body responded in kind. I curled closer to him. "But we all have strengths and weaknesses. I didn't realize word puzzles were one of your strengths."

I turned my face up, letting the sun warm it. I wanted nothing more than to snuggle up with my men and forget about this whole Lucifer business. Now that we'd all accepted we were a unit, I wanted to enjoy our nooky time.

That would have to wait, however, until after we kicked the devil's ass.

"It's not one of my many, *many* strengths," I said pointedly. "But it is one of yours. I can't describe what it felt like after that sex spell. How I could feel each and every one of you, lending me your powers, your minds." I blew out a breath, which, I decided, was much different that sighing. Less like a Victorian lady on a fainting couch and more like an athlete working on her air control. "I could hear your mind working out the puzzle and giving me the answer."

"It was strange for us, too," Dante said. "I definitely felt a little weaker, like part of my power had been sapped away."

"That's how you're supposed to feel after a good fucking." Gareth snorted. "I guess you've never experienced one of those before."

Okay, we were all together, but that didn't mean everything was chocolate and roses. My guys still sniped at each other, but it was coming from a place of love. Like a family who teases one other.

I was 99% sure it came from love, at least.

"And the second challenge?" Bane got us back on track. "Figuring out how many perfect square numbers there were between 1 and 500?"

I shrugged. "I heard your voice explaining the answer. And remind me never to take Arithmancy from you. I'll stab myself in the eye with my pencil if I had to listen to more math explanations."

"And the third?" he asked, his voice clipped.

I rubbed my palms on my jeans. "I already told you. I had to fight and kill someone. A fake someone."

"Was it a human, a witch, a shifter, fae...?" Pen scratched against paper as Bane scribbled down more notes.

I reached for my blindfold, but Gareth stopped me. "I want you to return on the path you just took."

I gripped his wrist. "But..." I swallowed. "It was you. I'm sorry, Gareth, but they made me fight an image of you. But it was your voice I heard telling me to end it, to strike the killing blow," I hurried to add. "It was your fighting spirit that gave me the power to win that challenge."

I really wanted this damn blindfold off. I needed to see what he was feeling. I wouldn't see it on his face, but I'd be able to tell if he was pissed if his tats were swirling crazily or just lazily wandering around.

He chuckled, the sound rich and throaty. It warmed me straight to my heart. "You took my head? Good job, pet." He ran his finger over my bottom lip as relief flooded me.

"Was there any other challenge?" Dante asked.

"No." I nipped the tip of Gareth's finger. "Just those three."

Gareth gripped my shoulders and turned me around. He smacked my butt. "Find your way back."

I stumbled forward and rubbed my ass. "Not cool," I threw over my shoulder. At least, not when we weren't in bed. But I'd leave that thought for later, when we could all explore the idea more fully. I stretched my hands out in front of me and took a step.

Dante stayed by my side. "But when you fought fake Gareth, you probably used my vampire speed or something, right?"

"Nope." Although that was an interesting idea. Could I move Flash-fast after our sex magic spell?

"I bet the power from my warlock side helped." He sounded more hopeful than certain.

I blew my cheeks out like a chipmunk then let the air out with a pop. "I'm sorry, Dante. I didn't use your magic." I reached out to pat his chest but slapped his chin instead. "Next time, though, I'm sure your powers will help me immensely."

Bane smothered a snort.

Gareth wasn't so polite. He roared with laughter.

I ignored the sounds of a scuffle breaking out behind me and concentrated on walking my imaginary floor-plan. When I reached the point where I was certain I had 'entered' LL, I stopped. "Well? Am I out?"

"Yes." Gareth grunted as the sound of flesh hitting flesh met my ears. "Son of a—" Whatever he said next was drowned out with heavy thumps.

I whipped off my blindfold, blinked in the bright sun, and finally focused my eyes on two of my lovers wrestling on the lawn. Dante had Gareth in a sweet leg lock, until the demon smashed his boot into Dante's face.

I shook my head.

"Boys. Right?" A red-striped carton of popcorn appeared under my nose.

"Hazel!" I threw my arms around my friend, knocking the popcorn from her grasp.

Quincy's hands shot out, and a circle of energy expanded from his palms, encompassing the flying popcorn and carton. I got in a couple more death squeezes on Hazel as he floated the popped kernels back into their container and summoned it to his hand.

Hazel wedged her elbow under my ribs. "You have to learn how to hug without suffocating people," she said grumpily, but her lips fought a smile. She stepped back. "I hear you got the Root. Impressive." She jerked her thumb at the tumbling mass of arms and legs that was heading toward us. "Though why I had to hear it from that idiot instead of you, I don't know."

Heat rose to my cheeks. I should have called Hazel and Quincy. I gave him a tight squeeze while I delayed answering, stealing some popcorn in the process. But Hazel would have asked about every detail, including the spell we'd used to enhance my powers. We were friends, besties even, but there were some things I didn't want to tell her and that she wouldn't want to know.

Namely, the foursome I'd had for the sex magic spell.

"Things are crazy." I popped a bit of buttery goodness into my mouth. "And besides, I thought if I called, then you'd want to help with our attack on Lucifer. Sadly, that is a one-woman job."

"Oh, we're going to help." She grabbed my hand and swiped the rest of the popcorn from it. She crunched noisily. "We're going to help the shit out of this plan."

I looked at my empty hand then pointed at Quincy. "The carton is right there."

We side-stepped as Dante and Gareth rolled through. I winced as Gareth's nose hit Dante's elbow.

Hazel snatched the popcorn from Quincy's hand.

"Hey!" he said.

She ignored him and turned back toward the academy. "Quincy and I are back to help you end this, understand?"

I trotted after her, trying, and failing, to get some more popcorn. "But—"

"No buts." She shook her head, her black page boy swinging. "We are going to help you execute your plan to perfection. Just as soon as we know what it is."

Chapter Twenty-Six

I had a family-sized bag of lime-flavored tortilla chips in the center of my crossed legs. Unlike some people, I was kind enough to share. I shot Hazel a pointed look, but she was too busy poring over the floorplan Gareth had drawn up to notice.

We were back in Dante's room, or our communal room as I'd come to think of it. It did have the biggest bed after all. We'd just finished running down our plan for Hazel and Quincy and she was examining it from every angle, looking for flaws.

I handed Quincy the bag of chips. He sat on the floor next to me, both of us leaning back against the sofa.

"How's her mom doing?" I asked quietly.

"Good." Quincy grabbed a Diet Coke from the coffee table and handed it to me before getting himself a water. "They didn't want us to come, but I think..."

"That they're proud of you, too." I rested my head on his shoulder. What parents wouldn't be proud of them. Hazel and Quincy were amazing. I was proud to have them as friends.

And tomorrow we were going to either end Lucifer's threat or die trying. Of course, we were launching our assault at an ungodly hour. 4:17 am to be exact. That was the moment when the wards around LL would cycle and go down. I had one second to slip into his home or else get zapped out of existence.

And getting inside was the easy part of our plan.

Since only one person could slip in unannounced, so to speak, and because I was the only one of our quartet who the others were willing to perform sex magic on to combine powers, I was the lucky one chosen to sneak in, find Lucifer, draw blood, and steal his powers.

Yeah, it sounded bat-shit crazy to me, too. The odds of success were astronomically low. But if the sex spell worked like before, I'd feel confident tomorrow morning.

Everyone else was going to surround the palace, laying protective shields and fighting off any demons that might try to come to Lucifer's aid. They'd look for a way to take down Lucifer's wards so they could join me inside.

Neither Gareth nor Bane seemed optimistic they'd find a way to bring the shields down, but it gave them something to do. I much preferred being the one invading LL. I couldn't imagine how I'd feel standing around outside while someone I loved went up against the devil.

I eyed the bag of chips. I should probably eat healthy today, give myself lots of energy for the fight tomorrow.

I grabbed a handful of chips and shoved them all in my mouth. Screw that. I didn't want to spend my possible last day alive eating *granola*.

"Are you ready?" Quincy asked in a low voice.

"As I'll ever be."

"If you two would stop stuffing your faces, maybe we could go over the plan another time." Hazel crossed her arms over her chest and tapped her foot, looking like the cutest military dictator ever.

"We've gone over it to infinity and beyond." Planting a hand on the sofa, I pushed to standing and shook out my legs. "There's comes a point where you can be over-prepared."

Bane pursed his lips. "No," he said, "there really can't."

"The plan I've heard so far is a suicide mission." Hazel swallowed. "You can't go in there alone, Delaney."

"Um." I shifted my weight, my cheeks heating. "We've found a way for me to borrow some of the guys' powers temporarily. It will be like all four of us going in."

"What spell?" Hazel asked.

I pulled Quincy up and shook my head. "Just a spell."

Quincy strolled to Hazel and offered her some chips. He bobbed his chin at her.

"Yeah." Hazel munched on one of *my* chips. Like I said, I was a sharer. "Why limit it to four? Borrow Quincy's and my powers, too."

I grimaced. I knew they were trying to be helpful, but...eeew. "No, I'm good. This spell, uh—"

"Has a limit," Bane interjected smoothly. "A witch can't take more than three...contributions."

"Hmph." She didn't look like she believed us, but she let it go. "So, we all travel to lower world and surround Lucifer's home. Delaney breaches when the wards go down. And, what, creeps up behind him with a knife, cuts him and drinks his blood?"

"Pretty much." Dante ruffled his hair. "We're hoping for the element of surprise."

"We're hoping we get lucky," Gareth said.

"Thanks for the vote of confidence." I scowled.

"Much of this plan depends on your ability to be stealthy." Bane shook his head sadly. "If we had any other options, we'd use them."

"I can be stealthy!"

Five pairs of eyes blinked at me.

My shoulders dropped. Okay, maybe ninja-quiet wasn't at the very top of my skillset, but really, all I needed to do was get in front of Lucifer and get a little of his blood. And I was good at drawing blood.

Bane glanced at his watch. "It is getting late and we have an early start. I'd suggest we all go to bed." His gaze latched onto mine, pointed and hot.

My body warmed. My bed tonight would be shared with my three guys. We'd agreed to get a couple hours of sleep before casting our spell. If I had to wake up crack-of-ass early, three hot men pleasuring me was going to be the best of alarm clocks.

"Good idea." I cleared my throat. "Your rooms should be just as you left them," I told Hazel and Quincy.

Hazel strode to the door and pulled it open. She arched an eyebrow. "You coming?" she asked me.

"Not right now." I tapped a rapid tattoo on my thigh. I looked at the obnoxiously huge bed that dominated Dante's room. Right now I wanted nothing more than to bury my head under its blankets.

Hazel followed my gaze. Her face cleared. "Oh." One edge of her lips quirked up, and I knew she'd figured it out. My face burned. "Well, sleep tight. We'll see you in the morning."

Quincy tossed a wave over his shoulder before Hazel closed the door behind them.

I dropped my forehead into my palm. "Oh my God, she knows."

"Does that matter?" Dante asked.

I stumbled to the bed and threw myself on it, face down. "Izzut samma no."

Bane ran his hand up my leg. "What was that?"

I turned my head. Another hand settled on my low back and rubbed circles into it. My muscles relaxed. "In the grand scheme of things, no." If we survived all this, I wanted to live with all three of my men, and I wasn't going to ask two of them to hide in the basement of whatever fabulous mansion we ended up in.

But I'd kind of hoped that people would assume they were my lodgers, or something.

Gareth leaned back against the headrest and dragged me up so my cheek rested on his chest. "Sleep. We have a big day tomorrow." He lowered his head and kissed the corner of my mouth. The touch was so gentle from my demon, it made something deep inside of me melt.

"But before that, we have an even bigger morning." He rolled me so I was half-pinned by his weight.

Dante and Bane crawled onto the bed next to me.

Gareth squeezed my hip. "And you are going to need all the shut-eye you can get to be ready for us."

Chapter Twenty-Seven

"The ward is going to cycle in ten seconds." Gareth's voice was a low whisper in my ear.

I shivered. I loved his voice. Deep. Rough. It brought to mind every dirty thing the four of us had done in Dante's bed not two hours ago.

I shifted. This was the problem with sex magic. It enhanced me with some of their powers, yes, but it also lent me part of their sex drives, too. There was no other reason why I'd be thinking about each and every one of my men sliding into me instead of the monumental task of—

"Go." Gareth placed his palm on my back and shoved me through an open window just as the air around the palace sparked.

I tumbled forward, my knee banging onto the low stone sill. I glared back at my demon through the large arched window.

"You will stay alive," he ordered me. "You will return to us." He gave me one last hard look before disappearing around the corner to take his place on the perimeter.

I nodded even though there was no one to see it. I had to return to my guys. Anything else was unthinkable.

I hefted my backpack higher on my shoulder and examined the large Italian-style courtyard. LL was constructed like a Tuscan villa, though on a much larger scale. The sky above me was a burnt orange color, and the edges of the earth-colored stone walls seemed to melt into it.

I closed my eyes, ignoring the sweet scents of the tropical flowers that filled the patio. I visualized the floorplan. Twenty paces forward there should be a door that led inside. I opened my eyes and counted off my steps. Nothing seemed strange. Nothing distracted me, contrary to Gareth's warnings. The door was right where it should be and the handle eased down without a hitch.

Hmm. I'd thought I'd have to walk through some walls. Or take the leap of faith à la Indiana Jones with a disappearing floor. Why the heck had I memorized each and every step if the house was just as it appeared? But, because I had Gareth inside me, nagging me to stick to the plan, I visualized the path I'd take from my mental map and crept forward.

The air was cool on my skin, and I stifled a giggle that hell would be air conditioned. Though Gareth had been quick to tell me that lower world wasn't like how humans conceived it. But Lucifer ruled over lost souls, so it wasn't *unlike* our conception, either.

I hesitated at a set of wide, glass double doors, and peeked inside. When I saw it was empty, I darted past.

Then backtracked a few steps.

"Wow," I whispered. Now, that, was an amazing pool. It had a slide plunging down from a rock formation in the center and—I rocked onto my toes—yep, a lazy river twisting around the edges of the faux lagoon.

I looked at a cabana that I just knew had a bikini in my size and back down the hall where I was supposed to go.

I grumbled, deep in my chest. Rats. I forced my feet to move away from the pool. Maybe I could go for a dip after stealing Lucifer's powers.

The next arched doorway led to an entertainment room. A huge, micro-thin TV hung before a twenty-foot sectional sofa. I couldn't resist popping in and running my hand over the creamy leather. The cushions were deep, just like I liked them, and there was enough room for me and all my guys to spread out. And were those...?

Holy crap, the sofa had cup holders. Cup holders! I pressed a button on the armrest. And heaters.

I might have moaned a little. I'd never wanted a piece of furniture more.

Wood creaked outside the room, and I darted to the door, pressing my back against the wall. Damn it, I needed to focus. I peered down the hall and saw a short demon scuttle around the corner, carrying a silver tray. I gave one last longing look at the sofa and eased back onto my path.

I turned the opposite corner the demon had gone and went up the half staircase at the end of the hall. So far, my internal maps matched the actual floorplan exactly. If—

I paused. Sniffed. And tip-toed up to the next doorway.

I muffled a groan. It just wasn't fair. A huge dessert buffet lay spread out on a twenty-foot table. The centerpiece was a chocolate fountain with heaps of luscious looking fruit surrounding it.

My mouth watered. Maybe I had time for just a small snack.

Stop fooling around and move your ass. Gareth's voice in my head was as loud as if he'd stood before me. His discipline surged through my veins.

I wanted to argue. A little noshing session wouldn't take long. But Gareth had lent me some of his will-power. The least I could do was use it.

I wasn't happy about it, though. I might have stomped a little louder than I should as I returned to the hallway.

LL was the farkin' bomb, and I was a little bummed that an evil demon got to live here while my last apartment was a 300 square foot dump. Corruption really did pay. I would never—

Stop whining and use your brain. The Bane in my head sighed. *Do you truly think everything you desire just happens to be in Lucifer's home by coincidence?*

My steps faltered. Damn. He was right. And why couldn't I always be this smart. Lucifer's house was one big honey trap, and I was the bee. No, bear. Bees made honey; bears liked honey. But I'd rather be a honey badger, those things were fierce. They must like honey, too. It was in their name af—

Delaney. Magic Bane looked heavenward. *Concentrate.*

I breathed deep and channeled Bane's focus. I let his energy flow through me, centering my racing thoughts.

I could be scatterbrained, but this was next-level ditzy. This had to be some lower world magic, messing with my head. It was a good thing I had the essences of two task-masters humming under my skin. If I had been going this alone, I would be shoveling an entire cake into my face while watching Netflix right about now.

Maybe that's why Dante's strength hadn't helped me yet. He was too nice to nag me, even in a sex magic spell.

I climbed another set of stairs, shaking my head at my idiocy. A pool, an awesome couch, and a buffet had been enough to lure me from my purpose. I nibbled my bottom lip and turned onto a thickly carpeted hallway.

I couldn't ignore it anymore. Not only did I have a bitch inside of me who liked to go homicidal at times, but she was a basic bitch.

Sophisticated is something I would never be.

On the plus side, I was easy to please.

I passed a ten-foot-high oil portrait of Lucifer, posing with a statue of Aphrodite. Another one of him being fed grapes alongside a weird, goat-like creature.

Pan, Bane corrected me.

Soft clicks greeted my ears, and I pressed my back against the wall. The sounds came from the room ahead on my right. I checked with the map in my head and nodded.

That was it. Lucifer's study. And if I wasn't mistaken, those clicks were his hooves tapping against a tiled floor.

I pulled my backpack around to my front and eased the zipper open. I pulled the Root from it, clutching it in my left hand, and placed the bag on the ground. I wouldn't need it anymore. I pulled an athame from the waistband of my jeans and took one step forward.

Deep breaths, I told myself. This wasn't a problem. Sneak up behind him, give him a small cut, and scrape the blade on the rim of the chalice.

Then drink the blood.

Bile rose up my throat. That part grossed me out the most. It really should have been Dante's job. He liked blood, or at least he liked mine.

I took another step. I focused on the essences of all my men, swirling through me. I could do this. *We* could do this.

I glanced into the room. A gold-framed mirror took up most of the far wall. In its reflection, Lucifer stood in front of his desk, reading a document lying on its surface, his palms planted on the sturdy oak top.

I rolled onto the balls of my feet. It was go-time. I'd never get a better chance.

I crept into Lucifer's study, stealing up behind him.

He tapped one of his hooves on the ground, like he was impatient for me to get it over with.

Quickly now. Don't hesitate.

I nodded at the Gareth in my head and raised the athame. Over Lucifer's furry lower half, there was a lot of bare skin to choose from. I zeroed in on the meaty part of his triceps and slashed.

My blade sliced through nothing. The image of Lucifer wavered then disappeared, leaving me off-balance and with a sinking stomach.

My hip hit the desk. Ignoring the jab of pain, I spun, athame raised in front of me.

Lucifer lounged on the super awesome sofa that had been transported to this room. Unless he had two. Now I really was jealous. He kicked his hooves up on a matching ottoman, a smile stretching from ear to ear. "You didn't really think that plan would work, did you?" He tilted his head. "You did? Aww, that's cute."

"The day's not over yet." Okay, that was kind of a non sequitur, but he got my meaning. I threw the blade at him, using my magic to guide its path. I'd get one little cut then bring the athame back—

Lucifer plucked the knife from the air. "I'm beginning to sense some hostility from you, little one." He sighed dramatically. "I'd hoped we could be friends, but if that's the way you want to have it." He snapped his fingers.

The lush furnishings melted away, except for Lucifer's sofa. The paintings disappeared, as did the mirror and the large banana tree in the corner. The tile beneath my feet became rough stone. The walls lost their paint, their plaster, and became thick blocks of granite.

And everyone important to me in the world was manacled to those walls.

I sucked in a sharp breath. Hazel and Quincy were chained on the left wall, Bane, Dante, and Gareth each attached to the other three. The iron around their wrists looked hard, unbending, and the chains attached were inches thick.

Lucifer's study had become a dungeon, and we were all trapped inside.

Sweat slickened my palms, and I adjusted my grip on the Root. Even the temperature control seemed to have disappeared. "This is more like what I thought hell would be like," I muttered.

Lucifer inclined his head. "I try to meet expectations." He tapped the blade of the athame against his lips. "Well, now that we're all here, let the fun begin."

Chapter Twenty-Eight

I sprinted to Hazel and tugged at her manacle. "Are you okay?"

She gave me a look. "I'm chained to a wall in lower world. Not my best day."

My laughter turned a tinge hysterical, and I swallowed it down. I centered myself, felt my energy flow through me, and attacked the lock on the manacle.

Nothing.

"My magic is better than yours," Lucifer sing-songed.

I glared at him over my shoulder. I really hadn't thought the devil would have such a juvenile sense of humor.

"There's magic in the manacles," Hazel whispered. "It prevents us from using our powers, and I guess is shielded against yours."

Of course there was, because that's just how this day was going.

"It's going to be okay, Delaney," Quincy said. "We'll get out of this."

I nodded. His confidence was contagious. Either that, or the energy of all my men flowing through me zapped away my fear. "Yes. I'll—"

The Root of Corruption quivered, then was yanked from my hand.

I snatched for it, but it floated away, into Lucifer's outstretched claws.

He raised an eyebrow. "I haven't seen this for a very long time. And now you've brought it to me. How nice."

Son of a bitch. My skin flushed. My nostrils flared. "Give it back." It was a stupid thing to say. Of course, he wouldn't hand it over. But rage interfered with clever comebacks. I welcomed the emotion. I fed off it.

The bitchy witch inside of me raised her head and stretched.

Growling, I charged, bits of stone grinding to dust beneath my sneakers with each step.

Lucifer waved his hand, a wave of energy shooting forth.

I batted it aside and leapt.

We went down in a tangle of limbs and hooves. The Root hit the ground and rolled out of reach. Heat shot from my hands as I clasped Lucifer's head, squeezing.

He roared, his skin smoking. He pulled his legs up under me and kicked out, sending me flying.

I hit the wall. Hard.

Dante stared down at me. "Get up!" He struggled against his bonds. "He's coming."

I staggered to my feet. I met Lucifer in an explosion of fists and magic. We punched a hole in the ceiling. Left gouges on the floor. Hazel shrieked, ducking from a ball of fire. I fought through my fatigue and used everything in my arsenal to take the devil down.

We were equally matched. At least, we were now, with my bitch power and those of my three men. But it wasn't enough. The fight didn't end. Just kept going, on and on. It probably wouldn't stop until we both collapsed from exhaustion.

I clawed my nails into his face, aiming for an eye. Magic punched into my gut, sprawling me backwards.

And right next to the Root.

Blood dripped from my fingers. Some of it had to be Lucifer's. I grabbed for the chalice, snatching it up, and—

"You might want to put that down." Lucifer's voice was ice. He snapped his fingers. Five demons popped into existence, each standing next to one of my friends and lovers. Each holding a knife to their throats.

I lowered the Root to the floor with a clank.

"Do it, Delaney." Bane winced as the knife bit into his neck. "Save the world, not us."

A noble statement, but they *were* my world. And I wasn't in the habit of sacrificing others, even if it was for the greater good.

I pushed to my feet. But I could sacrifice myself for those I loved. "Let them go and I won't fight you anymore. I'll kneel quietly as you take my head." Well, probably not quietly. Once Hazel, Quincy, and my guys were safely out of lower world, I'd go back to fighting.

It wasn't honorable to go back on my word like that, but what can I say? A lie told to save my life and others seemed more in the white lie range of deceptions.

"Your head?" Lucifer tutted. "Why would I want to kill such an exquisite creature? No, it isn't your head I want."

"Run." Gareth glared at me, like he was trying to force his will with just his gaze. "Now."

I all but rolled my eyes. It was like he didn't know me at all. "What do you want?" I asked Lucifer.

He raised his hands. "Nothing you should object to. I offer you a partnership. A place by my side as I bring order to the worlds."

"And money into your pocket." There were many tyrants who thought their harsh measures were necessary to make the world a better place.

Lucifer wasn't one of them.

He laughed, the sound much too alike to Gareth's for comfort. "The peace and order will be a nice side benefit then. Join me, and you'll be safe and prosperous for the rest of your life."

"I just have to let you take over the magical world." I huffed. "Not going to happen."

"Let me make your options clearer." Lucifer crossed his arms over his chest. "You can either put a little bit of your blood into the Root of Corruption and hand it over to me or you can watch all of your friends die. What will it be?"

"Delaney, no. You can't give up your powers." Dante wheezed as his demon punched him in the gut.

My chest squeezed. No, I couldn't. Somehow that seemed worse than giving Lucifer my head.

I looked at Hazel and Quincy. At Bane and Gareth and Dante. And I couldn't let them die, either.

"It won't be so bad." Lucifer circled around me. He ran his fingers over my ponytail. "You'll awaken as a human. No powers, but no pain. You'll have your little life, your friends, and two lovers. An existence most humans could only dream of."

My shoulders drew back. "Two lovers?"

"My spawn betrayed me. A demon of the Asom realm. Of course I'm going to kill him." He sniffed. "But I'll spare the others. If you give me what I want."

I locked gazes with Gareth, the backs of my eyes burning.

"No one else has to die," Lucifer continued. "You can stop all the fighting, the wars. You can save all those lives with just one small cut."

Sacrifice Gareth. He wanted me to let Gareth die.

My demon nodded to me, giving me a permission I didn't want. He was willing to die, but I wasn't willing to let him.

My mind whirred, looking for an out. Searching for anything that would keep everyone alive.

I straightened my spine. It might have been imaginary Bane whispering in my ear. It could have been that I actually had a good idea of my own, for once. Either way, I knew what I had to do.

"All right." I picked up the Root and held it out to Lucifer. "I accept your terms."

Chapter Twenty-Nine

"Delaney, no!" Bane shook his head, his eyes blazing. "You're the Chosen One. You cannot do this."

"It's not worth it." Dante strained against his chains.

I looked at each of my loved ones in turn. Each with a blade to his or her throat.

There was no other option.

I released my grip on the chalice as Lucifer snatched it from my hand in triumph. He tossed me a blade. "I'll let you decide where to draw blood."

How generous of him.

I squared my shoulders. I could do this. I had a plan. And, if it didn't work, well, I'd spent most of my life as a human. I could go back to being magicless.

My inner witch howled, and I had to agree. Rationally, I knew I could be human again, but emotionally, I couldn't fathom the idea. My magic was a part of who I was.

I held the athame over my hand, the tip quivering.

Gareth growled, the sound thrumming through my body. None of my men wanted me to do this. They valued me more than their lives.

I brought the knife to my hand.

Which was why I had to do it.

I pressed the edge of the blade into my palm. Watched as the metal dented my flesh. I told my other hand to make a quick slicing motion.

My hand didn't move. I pressed harder, but I needed a cut to break skin and I couldn't bring myself to do it.

"Well?" Lucifer tapped a hoof. "I'm waiting."

I pulled the blade away and jabbed it in his direction. "This is harder than it looks in the movies, buddy. I'm having a mental block about harming myself." Seriously, all those witch movies where they made blood oaths were bullshit. People don't casually cut holes into their skin, not even small holes. At least not normal people. Our instinct for self-preservation was too great.

"Oh, for fuck's sake." Lucifer snatched the athame, grabbed my wrist, turning my hand palm up, and made a quick slice.

A ribbon of blood bloomed across my hand, followed by a sharp sting.

He turned my hand over the Root, licking his lips as my blood dripped into the chalice.

A wave of dizziness swamped me. I staggered, Lucifer's grip on my wrist the only thing holding me upright. Nausea pulsed in my stomach with every drop of blood that splattered against the gold cup.

Lucifer tossed me aside, and I plopped onto my butt. The cool stone beneath me felt good against my heated skin. I blinked, looking up, trying to make my eyes focus as one of the best parts of my life was taken away.

Lucifer raised the chalice to his lips and tipped it back.

I moaned as something deep inside me tore away.

Dimly, I heard Gareth howl. Lucifer chuckle. Someone wail. It sounded like Hazel, but that didn't make sense. She wasn't a crier.

My face was pressed against the floor, the rough stone abrading my cheek. I pushed up to sitting and rubbed at the sting. It was the only thing on my body that hurt. The flu-like symptoms had disappeared. I felt nothing.

Was nothing.

Except a regular human.

My magic was gone.

I stood, unable to meet the gazes of any of my men. "Our deal?" I said to Lucifer.

He waved his hand. Every demon except the one at Gareth's side disappeared.

That helped the odds. "You're actually going to let the others go?"

"Of course." He eyed the Root, then Bane. "I'm a businessman. How many people would want to come to an agreement with me if they learned I don't keep my word. But I'm still a wee bit thirsty." He swaggered toward my professor, dismissing my presence.

I forced myself not to fling my body in front of Bane. Without my magic, the action would be less than useless. I closed my eyes. Focused. Now wasn't the time to merely react. Now I had to see if my crazy-ass plan could work.

I need ideas, I told the Bane, Gareth, and Dante in my mind. *The Root took away my magic, but it didn't touch yours.*

Even through my grief at losing my powers, I couldn't deny I was pretty damn proud of myself for this idea. Lucifer hadn't known that my guys had lent me some of their powers, and the Root only took the magic of the person whose blood was in the chalice. Until the sex magic spell wore off, I still had some fight left in me.

The powers we lent you from the three of us are probably enough to make about one moderately powerful witch, Bane said. *You can't take Lucifer on directly.*

The real Bane laughed bitterly at something Lucifer said. Engaged him in further conversation. He would delay Lucifer stealing his magic for as long as possible, I knew.

A summoning spell. Dante planted his hands on his hips. *We have enough power for that.*

What is it you want more than anything right now, pet?

I considered it, and the answer became clear. My lips curved. I knew just the thing. *Let's do this.*

It was strange. Without my magic to channel it, Dante's, Bane's, and Gareth's spell pulsed through me like the zaps you get from static electricity. The sounds of their chanting rose in my head, crowding out the real world. *Hurry,* I begged.

I couldn't let Bane lose his magic, too.

Something long and hard filled my fist.

My eyes shot open. Holy. Shit. It had worked. I swung my battle axe in a wide arc, a grin stretching my lips.

The demon guarding Gareth took the knife from his throat and pointed it at me. "Hey—"

I leapt forward, swinging. The blade lodged in his neck and upper chest before he could say anything else.

Lucifer turned.

Relief swamped me. He hadn't cut Bane yet. Thank God the devil was chatty.

He took a step toward me. "You dare?" His voice thundered through the chamber, echoing off the stone walls.

"Of course." What was it with demons and daring? Dak had said the same thing to me. Right before I'd killed him.

I heaved the axe over my shoulder, bringing it down on the lock on Gareth's manacle. It sheared off, and Gareth yanked free. Using his unfettered hand, he sent a zap of magic to pop the other lock open.

I rested the axe handle on my shoulder. "I'm Delaney Giantslayer Jones. And you're going down." My inner bitch may have been declawed, but I still had her attitude.

Lucifer launched a ball of fire at my head.

Gareth stepped in front of me, throwing up a shield. "Go." He nodded at Dante. "Free him, too. I'll deal with my father."

And with a primal roar, Gareth charged Lucifer.

I darted to Dante, taking aim at the manacle.

He closed his eyes as I swung the axe, breathing a sigh of relief when his hand popped free with only the tiniest of cuts. He grabbed the back of my neck and drew me to him for a hard kiss. "How...?"

"Fight now." I sprinted across the room toward Hazel and Quincy. "Explanations later," I called over my shoulder.

A chunk of ceiling crashed to the floor at my heels. A favorite move of Lucifer's, I thought darkly, thinking of Ophelia. But I trusted Gareth and now Dante to keep me safe from Lucifer's attacks.

"Did you switch it?" Hazel asked as I freed her. "Give Lucifer a fake Root of Corruption?"

"Nope." I knocked the lock off of Quincy's manacles. "I am officially no longer a witch."

"Then how—"

Quincy rubbed his wrists. "You know."

Her face cleared. "The sex magic spell. You're on borrowed powers."

"Sheesh, could you say that any louder?" I stomped along the wall toward Bane, shoulders hunched toward my ears. I didn't need *everyone* knowing my business.

"Hello, sweetheart." Bane held his manacle out from the wall as far as it would go. The sympathy in his voice almost broke me. He'd figured out what I'd done. Knew that in a few short hours I'd be completely magicless. A Muggle.

I hacked at his locks, the backs of my eyes burning.

He shook out his arms then reached for me. He kissed me softly. "When this is over, we are going to have a long talk about you sacrificing your magic over our wishes." He patted my butt. "A very long talk."

A shiver raced down my spine. I raised my mouth again to his.

Bane shoved me down, a stream of magic flowing over our heads. "Take cover. Stay down until we've finished." He rose and ran into the fight.

"Sure," I said into empty space. "I'll just stay here and—"

A demon popped into existence next to me.

I swung my axe. My leverage wasn't good from my knees, but there was still one less of Lucifer's minions when I was done. "—and kill demons."

Hazel and Quincy trotted toward the battle in the center of the room, but pulled up short when three more demons apparated in front of them. Hazel hit them with a freezing spell, and she and Quincy circled the new statues.

Only to stop when more demons appeared in the room.

A glint of silver caught in my peripheral vision, and I side-stepped out of the way of the knife swinging at my face. The demon holding it leered at me, one of his friends circling to my right.

I held up my hand, calling on my borrowed magic to throw up a wide shield. It wavered, shimmered, barely holding.

I swallowed. The essences of my guys were fading. I sent out some desperate, last blasts of magic, taking out a demon creeping up on Gareth. My next spell stunned a demon, but didn't drop him.

"Screw it." I twirled the axe. It was back to basic Delaney. I'd been happy fighting with my fists and human weapons mere months ago, and I would be again.

I charged a green, four-armed demon, dropping to a painful slide under its grasping hands, and sliced through its knee.

It was for the best that the sex magic spell was waning. My guys needed their full powers back to take down Lucifer.

The battle was ugly. Demon blood stung my eye, and I gagged a little thinking I might have swallowed some when I'd opened a vein of my last attacker. Hazel, Quincy, and I stood in a loose triangle, taking down every demon as they appeared.

"How many," Hazel said, grunting as she set the legs of her demon on fire, "of these damn things are going to appear? Hell has to run out of demons at some point."

I looked around at the strewn bodies. Thirty? Maybe forty? I was certain Lucifer had a heck of a lot more minions on call than that. I could only hope we ended this before he sent for middle world reinforcements. I couldn't deal with facing a room full of witches to kill.

"We have to cut the head off this snake." I looked at my battle axe. It dripped of gore. I had a feeling that saying was going to become very literal, very soon.

Hazel nodded. "Let's get you close."

We moved as one unit, backs turned toward each other, blasting and hacking anything that got in our way. Something with three malformed heads reached for me. I swung at the first neck. "That's for Killough," I yelled. Blood pumping, I took aim at the second. "And that," I said, tearing open its throat, "is for Ophelia."

The third head shrieked. I punched it in the nose. "And this is for me." I brought the axe down and back up like a golf club. It sliced through its abdomen, spilling guts, before lodging under its rib cage.

I panted, wiping the back of my forehead with my wrist. That kill had been way more satisfying than it probably should have been. My morals had definitely shifted. I glared at Lucifer. Something else to be pissed at him for. If he hadn't tried to take over the magical world, I never would have known that I could take some pleasure in killing things.

But only bad things.

Quincy threw a shield up in front of me as a stream of magic came my way. He nodded at something in the corner of the room. "Get it. We'll cover you."

I looked through Lucifer's furry legs and Dante's khaki-clad ones. The Root glinted in the light created from all the spells flying around the room.

My pulse raced. I could get my powers back, and more. The more kind of worried me. Did evilness come along with the devil's powers? But the risk was worth it to remain a witch. Lucifer was hurt bleeding; my men had seen to that. All I had to do was get the chalice, a little bit of his blood, and I was back in business.

And if we took Lucifer's powers, we could let him live. Gareth wouldn't have to lose his father.

I darted around a Masterna demon, rolled beneath a Glauxo. A stream of gold magic shot over my shoulder, taking out a half-shifted were man. I didn't waste time yelling 'thanks' to Hazel.

I put my head down, my eyes focused on the Root. Twenty more feet. Fifteen. I could almost feel the rush of power it would give me as it flooded my body. Ten. I was almost there. I was—

Something scaly crashed into me, knocking me over like a bowling pin.

It hissed, a forked tongue flicking across my cheek.

Quincy levitated it off of me, and threw it across the room.

I raised my hand in thanks as I staggered to my feet. And had to duck as Gareth's thick arm swung over my head, connecting with Lucifer's jaw.

He shoved me none too gently behind him. "Working here."

Dante and Bane shot twin spells, the arcs of energy piercing Lucifer's chest, and he fell back a step. Then straightened and hit my men with his own magic, tossing them ass over teakettle onto the stone floor.

I held my hand out toward the Root, beckoning it to come to me with a summoning spell. The chalice quivered, rolled an inch, then stopped. "Try crossing the streams." I panted, even that little bit of failed magic exhausting me.

Bane shook the pain from his expression and mouthed 'What?'

Clearly I wasn't the girl who had pithy one-liners during a fight scene. And I really needed to have an 80's movie night with all my men if we survived. Bane not picking up on my *Ghostbusters* reference was just sad.

Lucifer tipped his head back and roared. It looked like he was recharging himself from the inside out. He took a step toward Gareth, still lying on the ground.

And then it happened. That moment that comes only if you're damn lucky during a fight. The opportunity you have to seize if you want to win.

Lucifer slipped in a pool of blood, falling off balance to one knee.

I shot the chalice a split-second glance. The back of my throat burned for everything I was losing. For the future of magic I was giving up.

But magic wasn't the only thing I wanted in my future. I wanted Bane, and Dante, and Gareth. I wanted Hazel and Quincy to be able to finish school, have the lives they deserved. I wanted peace among the worlds, damn it.

Stiffening my spine, I hefted the axe over my shoulder.

Gareth caught my eye. Nodded.

Time slowed. My vision tunneled so only Lucifer remained in sight. He turned his head. His eyes stretched wide, those gold eyes that were so familiar.

My head went light. I'd seen this before. Done this before. That moment in the In-Between when I'd killed fake Gareth wasn't just a memory, but a foretelling.

Lucifer raised his hands to defend himself, but it was a moment too late.

My blade sliced through his skin, through his spine, and out the other side. The ruler of the lower world fell to the ground in two pieces.

I dropped my weapon, chest heaving. I turned my face away from the accusing expression on Lucifer's severed head and met Gareth's gaze. I took two steps and fell to my knees next to him, pressing my hand to the open wound on his side. "Are you okay? I'm so sorry I killed your dad. I—"

He cupped my cheek. "No looking back, pet. You did it. You saved the world." He shot a look at Lucifer's body, disgust flashing in his eyes. "I never thought anything could take him down. Or anyone."

The look he gave me, however, was filled with pride. I hated that I'd had to kill his father, but I wouldn't face any recriminations from Gareth. He was a warrior, and we were victorious. That was all my demon needed.

Dante squatted beside me. He ran his hands over my body, checking for injury, before pulling me in for a bear hug. "I can't believe it. You're alive. We're all alive."

I shook my head. I couldn't believe it, either. My adrenalin was still pumping, my hands were starting to shake, but it was over. We'd done it. We'd saved the magical world.

"But your powers—"

"No," I interrupted Dante. There would be a time to mourn my magic. A time when I'd need all my guys to hold me as I cried for my loss. But now wasn't that time.

We'd taken on the devil and won. Now was a time for celebration. And chocolate.

Bane knelt on my other side. He pulled my hand from Gareth before hovering his own over the wound. Healing magic streamed from his palms into Gareth's side. "The prophecy has been fulfilled. It's a shame Druella isn't alive to see it."

"The prophecy? Druella?" Who the hell cared about the prophecy at a moment like this? I rolled my eyes. My next task would be to loosen Bane up. It would be a challenge, but if I could take down Lucifer, I felt like I could pretty much do anything.

With help, of course.

I gripped the back of Bane's neck and drew his face to mine. When our lips met, I felt all the hunger, the relief, that my sexy and stodgy Brit didn't know how to express with words.

Hazel cleared her throat, and regretfully, I pulled back. I licked my bottom lip. I wanted a shower big enough for me and my three men so I could clean and kiss every inch of them.

"I hate to interrupt this touching moment," she said wryly, "but what are we going to do about all of this." She waved her hand around the room. Almost every square inch was covered with either a dead demon or.... I frowned. Kneeling demons?

"What's going on?" It was great all the minions had stopped fighting when Lucifer died, but their new stillness was just a bit creepy.

"You killed the ruler of lower world." Gareth inclined his head, a mock bow that was contradicted by a diabolical smile. "All its creatures now kneel to you."

I blinked. I opened my mouth to tell the demons to get up off their knees. That I wasn't suited to being the leader of anything, much less the underworld. But no speech came to me. No great words of wisdom that would solve this new mess I'd landed in.

I fell onto my butt and rested my back against Dante's shoulder. I only had one thought, and of course my lips opened before my brain could think better of it. "Fuck. My. Life."

Chapter Thirty

Dante dipped the juicy, red berry in the chocolate fountain and brought it to my lips.

The four of us were in Lucifer's bedroom, now mine, and I had to say, this underworld business didn't suck. I'd had hell's minions clean the palace from top to bottom, getting rid of corpses and all bodily fluids, plus the creepy art that we'd found in a secret room off the ballroom.

I shook the memory of those sculptures off. New linens on the beds and fresh coats of paints in cheery yellows and whites, and this place was looking less like Dracula's castle and more like Downton Abbey.

And with the chocolate fountain now lodged beside the immense bed that fit all four of us, it was just about perfect.

I still wasn't comfortable calling it home, however.

"Raven will be reopening in two weeks." Bane leaned against the headboard, shuffling through some papers. "Dreadmoon has asked me to be deputy headmaster."

I frowned. Since he could apparate, the commute wouldn't be bad, and I was happy Hazel and Quincy would get to return to school, but I didn't know how much I liked the idea of Sinjin returning to normal middle world life while I had to deal with sorting out lower world.

I was still trying to figure out how to step down from Lucifer's throne. Renouncing my title wasn't as easy as Prince Harry made it look. Paranormals took their royalty a bit more seriously.

Dante couldn't understand why I didn't want the job. He thought it was a great opportunity to reform lower world, make it a friendlier, safer hell.

Gareth spent every waking moment amping up my security, worried that some demon would put a target on my head in order to take over lower world.

Melted chocolate heated my upper thigh. Gareth leaned down and licked it off.

Well, almost every waking hour. We spent a lot of time in this bedroom.

A lot of time.

"There's a new spell I want to try." Bane frowned, pushing a pair of glasses up his nose. "The warlock I spoke with said if we found a dragon root plant that grows at an altitude over fifteen thousand feet, and take venom from a—"

I reached over and snatched his papers, tossing them to the floor. "We've tried a dozen spells. They aren't working." There weren't any spells that turned humans into witches. There were spells to augment power, transform powers, strip power, but nothing we could use. "I'm tired of wasting our time. I'd rather spend it on more pleasurable activities." I waggled my eyebrows as I slid my foot up and down his shin.

Dante rolled me to my back. "We could do the sex magic spell every morning." A sexy grin stretched his lips. "I think that's magic we could all get behind." He nuzzled behind my ear, his hand starting to wander.

I sank into the down mattress. It was tempting. Almost as tempting as Gareth's head as it settled between my thighs. But I didn't want to keep borrowing magic, magic that would never truly be mine. I'd be a virtual succubus. Or was it an incubus that drained a person's vitality? I shook my head. Either way, I didn't want to perpetually leach power from my guys.

"Let's save that spell for only when we need it." I rocked my hips into Gareth's tongue, my mind starting to get that lovely floaty feeling that only happened when my men worshipped my body.

"I suppose work can wait a couple more hours." Bane scooted next to me and turned my face to his, butterflying his lips across mine. He sucked my lower lip into his mouth, tugging gently, and I moaned.

And then my stomach growled.

Bane raised his head.

Dante stopped his hand from roaming.

Gareth pulled back. "I think our pet needs something more substantial than chocolate-coated fruit."

Dante rolled off the bed and pulled on his pants. "I'll pop out to that restaurant in New Orleans you like so much. Get you the chicken jambalaya."

"She said she wanted to try the bangers and mash from my favorite pub." Bane found his own clothes. "A portal is already set up there."

I frowned. Clothes were going in the wrong direction, on instead of off. "Guys, it's not important. I can grab a sandwich. After."

Gareth rolled a black tee down his beautiful chest, tucking it into his jeans. "The new cook here has been trained in her favorites. I'll tell him to grill her a juicy steak."

"But—"

"She'll like the jambalaya best." Dante planted his hands on his hips. "I'm getting it."

"You get what you want, pup." Gareth swaggered toward the door. "We'll see whose meat Delaney likes best."

Dante and Bane nodded and scrambled after him.

"But..." I blinked. The room was empty. All the lovely tingles that had been raised in my body fizzled out as my guys disappeared to hunt me down some grub.

I didn't know whether to be grateful that they wanted to see to all my needs, or pissy that they thought I'd prioritize my stomach over other parts of my body. A couple key parts in particular.

I rolled to my side and pulled the duvet up to my chin, huffing. Maybe it wasn't entirely their fault they made the wrong choice. I should probably work on not being so grumpy when I got hungry.

I yawned. I couldn't complain too much. Bane, Gareth, and Dante still hadn't settled fully into the idea of sharing, but their competitions and one-upmanships really worked in my favor. They tried to outdo each other in *every* aspect of our relationship.

Hazel and Quincy visited often, mainly to use the pool, but we were spending almost as much time together as when we were all at Raven.

I was now the owner of the most awesome couch ever created, and had three men I loved to snuggle up on it with as I made them watch all my favorite 80s movies.

I had a job, of sorts, and that was something a lot of high school dropouts couldn't say. The job entailed keeping thousands of demons and countless souls in line, but the benies were awesome.

There was only one thing missing.

I stared at my palm, tracing the lines where my magic used to flow from my body.

The past few days I'd felt...different. A little more pep in my step. A bit more optimism flowing through my veins.

I eyed the can of Diet Coke on the bedside table. Slowly, I reached out, my hand stopping inches from it.

I centered myself, searching for my inner bitch.

Something shifted inside of me. It didn't feel quite like my witch, but it was something. My demon side?

A bead of sweat rolled down my temple. My fingers ached. But finally, the can quivered. It might even have moved a millimeter. My shoulders sagged in exhaustion, and I flopped onto my back. But I was a happy-tired.

Scratch that, I was an elated, over-the-moon kind of tired.

It wasn't much, that little shimmy. Bane would probably say the can moving had been my imagination.

But I knew better.

It was a start.

About A. Caprice

A. Caprice is the pen name I use when I want to write something a little different. If it's magical, or furry, or has fangs, this is the name I'll write it under. There might even be aliens! I live in Colorado, home of many Big Foot sightings. I used to practice law, but decided I'd rather write about happy endings and forget the mess people can make of their lives. I also write humorous, small-town, contemporary romance novels under the name Allyson Charles and steamy historicals as Alyson Chase.

Printed in Great Britain
by Amazon